Tensions running high . . .

Once Devon had a seat, Maggie moved us away from the shore. I slid my paddle forward in the canoe so Devon could reach it.

"If you're sitting in the bow, you'll have to paddle," I told her.

Devon didn't touch the paddle. Instead she sat perched on the canoe seat, thumbing through her magazine while Maggie was busy paddling with all her strength in the stern.

"Devon, you have to paddle!" I yelled. "Stop reading and help out!"

"Yeah, Ghosty Girl. I'm doing all the work here," Maggie called from the stern. She swung her paddle forward and flicked the blade up so that droplets of water hit the back of Devon's shirt. "Come on, let's see some arm muscle."

Devon flinched a little when the water drops hit her, but she didn't turn around. "If I feel another drop of water on me, you'll be flossing your teeth with that paddle," she said coolly.

"Oh, yeah?" Maggie yelled. "How about I feed your magazine to the fishies?"

One Summer. One Sleepaway Camp.
Three Thrilling Stories!

Summer Camp Secrets

How far will Kelly
go to hold on to
her new friends?

What happens when Judith
Ducksworth decides to
become JD at camp?

Can Darcy and
Nicole's friendship
survive the summer?

TUG-OF-WAR

Summer Camp Secrets

TUG-OF-WAR

by
Katy Grant

ALADDIN
New York   London   Toronto   Sydney

For Michael

Con mucho amor, mi amiga
The magic genie publishing lamp finally worked!

ALADDIN
An imprint of Simon & Schuster Children's Publishing Division
1230 Avenue of the Americas, New York, NY 10020
First Aladdin paperback edition April 2010
Text copyright © 2010 by Katy Grant
All rights reserved, including the right of reproduction in whole or in part in any form.
ALADDIN is a trademark of Simon & Schuster, Inc., and related logo is a registered trademark of Simon & Schuster, Inc.
For information about special discounts for bulk purchases, please contact Simon & Schuster Special Sales at 1-866-506-1949 or business@simonandschuster.com.
The Simon & Schuster Speakers Bureau can bring authors to your live event. For more information or to book an event contact the Simon & Schuster Speakers Bureau at 1-866-248-3049 or visit our website at www.simonspeakers.com.
The text of this book was set in Perpetua.
Manufactured in the United States of America
0210 OFF
10 9 8 7 6 5 4 3 2
Library of Congress Control Number 2009905998
ISBN 978-1-4169-9161-8
ISBN 978-1-4169-9911-9 (eBook)

TUG-OF-WAR

Acknowledgments

My dear friend Michael Ramirez, author and play-wright, has been with me from the start of this series. We first met at an SCBWI conference in 1995. While I was having a manuscript critique of the novel that would later become *Pranked*, she waited for me outside the room to offer moral support. For this book, she helped me with the Spanish phrases, read an early draft, and as always, responded with prompt, insightful feedback. Over the years, she has been a great friend, critique partner, and, in many ways, my mentor.

Also, last year I was overjoyed to reconnect with an old friend from my own summer camp, Margaret Black. We have had a *ridiculous* amount of fun and laughs recalling our glory days through e-mails, phone calls, and photos. Her memory for detail rivals (if not surpasses) my own, and she has been an excellent resource for me while writing this book and the two that will follow it. Margaret and her daughter Betsy read an early draft of this book and provided feedback, something that thrilled me to no end, since Betsy now attends our old summer camp. Betsy is a third-generation camper, no less!

I also want to thank my eleven-year-old cousin, Sheldon Kappel, for help with writing the chess scene.

Sheldon has been playing for the past three years, and he competes in both individual tournaments and on his team at Lake Castle Slidell School. Sheldon was able to give this scene the air of authentic chess play that I could not.

And thanks to Liesa Abrams, whom I finally met face-to-face over lunch at Pizzeria Picasso. She has always helped to make the whole process smooth and easy, from the first grain of an idea all the way to the galleys. Now on to the next one!

CHAPTER 1

Sunday, June 15

Five minutes. We'd barely been at Camp Pine Haven for five minutes, and I was already tempted to push my best friend Devon into the lake.

We were standing on the edge of Lakeview Rock, this gigantic rock formation that loomed up over one end of the lake, giving us a great view of just about everything from up here.

Not only could we see the lake below us with the wooden dock sticking out over the water and the rows of canoes lined up on the banks, but we could catch a glimpse of the tennis courts nearby, slightly hidden by the trees.

Devon and I had just gotten off the bus, and since she'd hated every minute of the ride here, I decided

I'd give her a quick tour while our stuff was being unloaded.

Devon took a step closer to the edge and looked down, her arms crossed in front of her. We were about thirty feet high, I figured.

"I don't think this actually qualifies as a lake. Swamp, maybe. Why is it so green?" She crinkled her nose in disgust, as if the lake had a bad smell. It didn't.

Everything smelled wonderful up here—like pine trees and fresh air. I took a deep breath and got a whiff of wild honeysuckle from an overgrown vine growing around the trees below us.

"It's green because . . . lakes are always green." I thought the lake was a beautiful shade of green, not slimy or mossy. It was the same color as all the trees around it. There's absolutely nothing swampy about Pine Haven's lake.

A group of girls and parents were walking around the opposite side of the lake, and I strained my eyes to see if I recognized any of them. I couldn't wait to see my old friends, especially Maggie. I hadn't seen her since last summer.

Devon let out a bored sigh. "Okay, nice swamp. Let's go check out the pool now."

I gritted my teeth. "Devon, there is no pool. We swim in the lake. I thought you knew that."

She turned her head slowly and looked at me, her mouth slightly open. The expression on her face looked like I'd told her a gigantic, girl-eating kraken lived in those waters. "No pool? There's . . . *no* . . . *pool*." She emphasized each word carefully.

"How did you get the impression that Pine Haven has a pool?" I asked. "Didn't you look at the brochures I gave you? Or the website?"

Devon shrugged. "I might have glanced at the brochures once or twice, but when I went to the website and saw that there was a clock counting down the days till I'd be shipped off here . . ." She didn't even bother to finish the sentence.

Devon was wearing her two favorite wardrobe colors. She had on a black tank top and white shorts. I couldn't figure out why she dressed in black and white so much. Maybe because her hair was black and her skin was milky white. Next to Devon, my complexion was a warm caramel.

Personally, I made a point of never wearing black or white. Too blah for me. Today, for instance, I was wearing one red and one yellow Converse high-top. The best part about owning high-tops in assorted colors was that you could mix them up. As far as I was concerned, the more color, the better.

"Ready to see the rest of camp?" I asked.

"Chris, please wake me up from this nightmare. You can't be serious about there being no pool."

"Devon, are you trying to make me mad? Because you're succeeding," I warned her.

"Ooh, don't awaken the Hulk." Devon knew not to push me to the limit.

All my family and friends were well aware of my temper. My mom was constantly telling me I needed to learn to control it, but I figured everyone else should try not to make me mad in the first place.

"Continue with the tour," Devon said. "Any chance the Sistine Chapel is around the corner?"

We'd started walking through the trees, away from Lakeview Rock, when I stopped dead in my tracks and turned on her. "Are you going to spend the next four weeks complaining about your parents not taking you to Italy?" I snapped at her.

"Yes, that's exactly what I'm going to do. I still can't believe my parents are forcing me to spend an entire month at some backwoods girls' camp in North Carolina when I could be visiting the Forum or the Colosseum with them!"

That explained why Devon hadn't bothered to look at the stuff I'd given her about Pine Haven; she'd been too busy looking at all her parents' travel brochures.

"Devon, you're here at camp, so do us both a favor and try not to drive me insane."

Devon frowned. "Sorry. I'm not trying to drive you insane. The one good thing about this whole camp experience is that you're here with me, Chris. At least the two of us get to stick together the whole time, right?"

I smiled at her. "Right. Give Pine Haven a chance, okay? There might be some things you actually like."

We walked up the road to where the bus was parked.

I'd gotten this nervous feeling when Devon's mom called my mom a couple of months ago and asked about Devon coming to camp with me this summer. Yes, we're best friends, but Devon is not the outdoorsy type. I think she might be allergic to nature. But her parents had planned this big European vacation that didn't include her or her older sister Ariana, so Ariana decided on a music camp, and Devon got shipped off to Pine Haven with me. I really did like the idea of Devon coming to camp with me, but I knew it would take her a while to get used to things around here.

"Okay, back behind those trees at the top of that hill is the climbing tower. It's really cool. Kind of a combination climbing wall and wooden maze with netting and ropes and stuff. And this road leads through camp and down to the stables."

"Stables? You mean, like a barn? With cows?"

"No, not with cows! Horses. You know, for riding. Some people ride horses."

It seemed like there were even more people wandering around now than when we first got off the bus, and I kept looking for Maggie everywhere in the crowd of parents, counselors, and arriving campers. I yelled and waved at Erin Harmon, but we were too far away to actually talk, and anyway, she was helping Melissa Bledsoe carry her stuff up the hill toward the cabins. I was about to tell Devon that we should grab our stuff too, when I heard someone calling me.

"Chris! Christina Ramirez!"

Rachel Hoffstedder, my counselor from last year, was trying to get through the crowd of people still standing around the bus.

"Rachel!" I ran up and gave her a hug. Devon hung back a few steps and waited.

"Hey! You're the first old camper I've seen so far! Guess who you got for a counselor this year? Wayward!"

"Wayward? Awesome!" Caroline Heyward, aka Wayward, was a really cool counselor who'd been coming to Pine Haven since forever. "Who's my other counselor? What cabin am I in?" Devon made a little coughing sound at my elbow.

"Oh, sorry. Rachel, this is my friend Devon. This is her first year."

We'd barely gotten through that introduction when Laurel-Ann Hyphen came running up. She looked exactly the same as last year, with her hair in two long braids, but I noticed she had braces now.

"Hey, Chris! I'm in Cabin Four with you!" said Laurel-Ann. "But you're on Side A with Maggie Windsor and a couple of new girls. I'm on Side B. You've got Wayward, but I've got some new counselor who's never even been here before! A total newbie! Oh, and guess who else is on Side B with me? Boo Bauer. I don't think she likes me, but you know, whatever. I'll be nice to her. Have you seen Maggie yet? She's here. I just saw her."

It took me a couple of seconds to recover from Laurel-Ann's long hello. You never knew whether you should wait till she finally stopped talking or just jump right in anytime. "Ah, no. I haven't seen Maggie. Laurel-Ann, this is my friend Devon. I think she's probably one of the new girls on Side A with me."

I was completely blanking on Laurel-Ann's last name. All I could remember was that a lot of people called her Hyphen last year because she always made a point of telling everyone she spelled her name with one.

"Here, let's look at the cabin assignments," said Rachel. She checked the list on her clipboard and told us that Devon, Maggie, and I were all on Side A together, just like I'd requested.

"Well, I guess we should get our stuff and go to the cabin." I looked around for Devon, but she was already walking away from us.

Devon sat down on her new black trunk. On all sides of her, pillows, sleeping bags, and duffels were piled up in a semi-organized arrangement.

"Who was that obnoxious loudmouth with the braids?" she asked. "Tell me you're not friends with her."

"Don't worry. We won't be spending much time with Laurel-Ann—if we can help it. But I'm glad Maggie's here already. Wait till you meet her. She's got an insane sense of humor."

I scanned the pile of bags for my blue duffel. I wanted

to see Maggie, but I had this nervous feeling about how she and Devon would react to each other. Both of them had pretty unique personalities.

Devon opened her purse and pulled out a compact. Looking at the tiny mirror, she curled her mascaraed eyelashes with her finger, then dug around for her lip gloss, which she carefully applied, rubbing her lips together to smooth it all out.

I felt like telling her that nobody wore makeup at camp, not even the counselors, but I decided not to bother. She'd figure it out on her own.

She frowned and looked down at the trunk underneath her. "There is no way I'm carrying this thing by myself. It'll totally mess up my manicure." She inspected her nails for about the twenty-seventh time. She'd just gotten a French mani and pedi yesterday, and when I saw her nails this morning, I couldn't believe it. Who got a manicure the day before leaving for camp?

"Don't worry about it. Hey, guys, give us a hand?" I yelled to a couple of counselors from the boys' camp, Camp Crockett, who were standing around. One guy grabbed Devon's trunk and another took my duffel. We all started up the hill together.

"He's gorgeous!" Devon whispered, pointing to the dark-haired counselor.

"I noticed!" I whispered back. "Why don't you pretend to fall and fake a sprained ankle? He'll volunteer to carry you to the infirmary."

Devon smiled at me. "Great idea. Dare me to?"

We both laughed, and the guys glanced at us over their shoulders, breathing heavily from the load they were carrying up the steep hill.

I cleared my throat and acted serious so they wouldn't know we'd been drooling over them. "Okay, every cabin has eight campers and two counselors. The cabins are split in half, Side A and Side B. Up there at the top of the hill is Middler Line. That's what we are— Middlers. Ages ten to twelve."

"Middlers? We're called Middlers?" asked Devon. "How degrading. What are the people under us called? Lowlifes?"

"It goes Junior, Middler, Senior. We'll be Seniors next year when we're thirteen." I tried not to sound like a tour guide, but I figured she'd want to know all these different camp terms. I'd been pretty confused last year by all of them.

"The oldest campers are the CATs—they're sixteen. After that, you can be a CA—a Counselor Assistant."

"Cats?" asked Devon.

"Yeah. It stands for Counselor Assistant in Training.

Oh, down there's the dining hall, and on the porch are the mailboxes. Mail comes every day after lunch."

Now we were up on Middler Line, a wide dirt path with a long row of cabins in front of us. The Crockett counselors pushed through the screen door of Cabin 4.

"Oh, please." That was all Devon could say as she stood there looking around at the two big rooms full of empty bunk beds and bare wooden shelves.

I happened to like Pine Haven's cabins. Big screen windows let in plenty of fresh mountain air and sunlight. Above the screen windows were rolled-up canvas flaps that we could lower when it rained. The walls were bare, unpainted wood, and above us were rafters with a couple of lightbulbs to light the cabin after dark. Yeah, the cabins were basic, but they were comfortable.

"And they consider these accommodations fit for human habitation?"

The Crockett counselors left to go help other people with their trunks, but they were both snickering over Devon's comment.

I dragged my duffel over to Side A. "Devon, it's camp. I warned you it wasn't going to be the Hilton."

"Chris, I can live without the Hilton. But these are hovels."

She looked around at all the graffiti covering the

walls. "Was there a gang war we just missed? And where's the bathroom? Tell me there's not an outhouse out back we have to use."

I had to laugh at that. The thing I loved most about Devon was her sense of humor. She was constantly getting me in trouble at school because her sarcastic remarks always made me laugh out loud during class.

"You would've known about the outhouses if you'd looked at the website." Devon covered her face with her hands and groaned. "Do we get to use toilet paper? Or pine needles?"

"I'm just teasing you. We have real flush toilets with toilet paper and everything." I laughed as she recovered slightly from the shock I'd given her. "But they're not in the cabins. They're in another building down the line."

I figured Devon would freak when she saw Solitary. That was what everyone at Pine Haven called the bathrooms, for some random reason. It was basically one room with faucets all along the walls where you could brush your teeth and wash your face and stuff, and then there was an adjoining room full of toilet stalls.

Across the line from Solitary was a row of outdoor showers. They had stalls with doors on them and everything, but I knew Devon would be disgusted by them. We'd visit those later.

A girl I didn't recognize came in and stood in the doorway, looking a little lost.

"I'm supposed to be in Cabin Four, Side B," she said, dropping her sleeping bag at her feet.

"Okay, this is Side A, so you're on that side of the cabin," I told her, pointing to the opposite side. "I'm Chris, by the way. This is Devon."

"Hi, I'm Kayla." She glanced around at the beds on Side B.

"You can pick any empty bed you want," I called over to her.

"She looks about as thrilled as I am to be here," Devon whispered to me.

On our side of the cabin there were two sets of bunk beds, and I could see that someone had already taken one of the top bunks because the bed was made up with . . . Scooby-Doo sheets!

"Scooby-Doo sheets!" I yelled. Devon had no idea what I was talking about.

The next thing I knew, someone came crashing through the screen door, grabbed me, and spun me around in circles. I caught a glimpse of thick, rust-colored curls.

"Christina Kachina!" yelled Maggie.

"Windsoroni!" I screamed. We had each other in a

death-grip hug. When she finally turned me loose, I shot Devon a quick glance. She was glaring at both of us.

"Hey, Maggie, this is my friend from home—Devon Fairchild. Devon, this is Maggie—the maniac I've been telling you about."

Devon looked at us both and fluttered her eyelashes. "Oh, yes. Maggie. The maniac. Absolutely charmed to meet you."

CHAPTER 2

"Jeez, I hope you brought a gallon of sunscreen!" These were the first words out of Maggie's mouth when she saw Devon. It was really rude, but I knew she honestly didn't mean it that way. Thoughts had a way of popping into her head and draining out of her brain down to her mouth without ever stopping along the way. She had no control over the whole process.

She was looking Devon up and down. "You are one white kid! I've never seen anyone so pale!"

My mom says that with her silky black hair, blue eyes, and fair skin, Devon looks just like a china doll. At least she has sense enough not to say that in front of Devon.

"Do you fry like a slab of bacon in the sun? If you

didn't bring any sunscreen, you can use some of mine. I mean, I burn too. Look at these freckles." Maggie leaned forward to give Devon a good look, as if you could miss them.

"I have my own sunscreen."

I didn't *see* frost come out of Devon's mouth, but I felt it, and I'm sure Maggie did too. The whole cabin seemed twenty degrees colder.

"Oh yeah, I've got plenty too," I added. "So, which bed do you want, Devon?" Maybe if I distracted the two of them, things wouldn't get any worse.

She didn't answer. Now it was her turn to look Maggie up and down. "Did you raid your brother's closet? Or did your parents always want a boy?"

Maggie laughed. "Actually, I *did* raid my brother's closet!" She did a 360-degree turn to model the red Camp Crockett football jersey she was wearing. A Camp Crockett baseball cap was turned around backward, barely hanging on over her mass of dark red curls.

"Maggie's brother Jackson goes to Camp Crockett," I told Devon. "You'll meet him at the dances." I could hardly wait to see Jackson again. He was gorgeous. And I've been absolutely in love with him since I met him last year.

"Yeah, he's my big brother, so when I came along,

my parents were actually hoping for a girl. Think they were disappointed?" Maggie asked with a grin.

Devon stared at Maggie for about ten seconds without saying a word. Finally she asked, "Do you speak Spanish?"

"No, why?" asked Maggie.

"Good. *Mi gato se comió tu salchichas*."

"Hey, thanks!" Maggie answered cheerfully. "Same to you!"

I turned away from both of them, because I was choking on a laugh. Devon thought she'd just given Maggie the worst possible insult, when she'd actually said, "My cat ate your sausages."

Devon envied my being able to speak Spanish. She would love to be bilingual too, and she was constantly begging me to teach her Spanish, especially curse words. I usually taught her some random, meaningless phrase to make her happy.

One set of metal bunk beds was pushed against the front wall of the cabin, and the other was against the opposite wall. "Okay, let's figure out the sleeping arrangement. Maggie's obviously got one top bunk. Devon, you want bottom or top?"

Devon looked at the empty bunks and then back at me. "A bottom, of course."

Maggie sat down on the empty bottom bunk under hers. "Well, this one's for Chris. You can have the other bottom," she told Devon, pointing to the bunks on the far wall. Then she looked up at me and grinned. "Just like last year, huh, Chris?"

I unzipped my duffel and dug around inside for some clean sheets, acting like I hadn't heard her comment. Last year Maggie had the top bunk, and I'd had the bottom. It was great because we would whisper to each other for a long time after lights-out.

But now Devon was here. Maybe I should take the other top bunk so she and I could whisper together.

Devon opened her trunk and took out some plain white sheets to make up her bed. No Scooby-Doo for her.

"Want me to help you make up your bed, Chris?" Maggie offered. She glanced over at Devon, who kept banging her head on the springs of the top bunk above her and muttering under her breath, "*¡Sobacos!*" which just meant "armpits."

By now I'd pulled out my sky blue sheets with white clouds and rainbows all over them. It was time to make a decision. Lower bunk under Maggie or top bunk above Devon? I wondered if I had a quarter in my duffel someplace. I might have to flip for it.

But at that moment Wayward walked in with another

camper. Wayward was wearing sunglasses and this funky plaid hat like snowboarders wear. "Hey, Chris. How's it going?" she asked when she saw me, like we'd just seen each other five minutes ago instead of sometime last summer. I felt honored that she even remembered who I was.

"I guess you're Devon. This is Betsy Smith."

Maggie gave Wayward a stern look. "Where's your official Pine Haven polo, missy?"

Wayward had on a green T-shirt from some ski resort in Colorado and a pair of khaki shorts. It probably annoyed Eda, the camp director, that Wayward was only sort of following the counselors' dress code. All the other counselors had on white shorts and their matching green Pine Haven polos with a little pine tree on them.

"Don't know. It's probably around here someplace." She smiled slowly and looked around. "Oh yeah, name tags."

She picked up a pile of wooden tags lying on a shelf by her cot and passed them around to the four of us. Everyone was supposed to wear them for the first week, until we all got to know each other.

Devon held hers up by the plastic string. "Did beavers make these?"

They were little oblong slices of wood—they actually looked like someone took a chainsaw and sawed up a limb from a tree, because there was still bark all around the edges.

"So," said Wayward, "y'all do whatever you feel like . . . and I'll be back. Eventually. Be Zen." Then she walked out.

Devon and Betsy, the new girl, both stared at the screen door as it banged closed.

"You do realize we got *the* coolest counselor at Pine Haven, don't you?" I said.

"Be Zen," Devon said, and nodded approvingly. I could tell Wayward was the first thing she actually liked about camp so far.

Betsy smiled shyly at us, waiting for someone to show her what to do.

And now, since all the campers on Side A were here, I had to make a decision—whether to share bunk beds with Maggie or Devon.

Why couldn't we have ended up with some single cots instead of two sets of bunk beds? That way maybe I could've picked a bed in between Devon and Maggie.

When Betsy noticed that Devon was busy putting sheets on her bed, she hesitated for a few seconds and then opened up her trunk.

So I tossed my sheets and pillow on the top bunk

above Devon. "Betsy, do you want the bottom bunk under Maggie?" I asked, feeling Maggie's eyes on me.

She shrugged and smiled. "Sure, that's fine." She was kind of on the tall side, and her blond hair was cut in a short wedge and parted down the middle.

The thing was, I wanted the top bunk, and not because I thought Devon wanted me close by. I just preferred the top. But I didn't want Maggie to feel like I was deserting her for Devon. I definitely wasn't.

"Do you mind, Windsoroni?" I asked Maggie when she gave me a quick glance.

Devon looked up from where she was sitting on her bottom bunk. "Windsoroni? Is that anything like Beefaroni?"

"Windsor is Maggie's last name. She always called me Christina Kachina last year, so I call her Windsoroni."

Devon cupped her hands over her mouth and started heaving. Maggie jumped up. "You okay?"

"No, I'm not. Your stupid nicknames are making me seriously ill."

"Ah, jealous? Don't worry about that. You'll get your own nickname pretty soon." Maggie wrinkled her forehead thoughtfully. "How about Ghosty? Or . . . what was your last name? Fairchild? I got it!" Maggie snapped her fingers. "Palechild!"

Devon looked past Maggie at me. "Do you hear an annoying buzzing sound? At first I thought it was someone talking, but now I think it's a fly." She focused her gaze on Maggie. "Got a fly swatter, Chris?"

"Oh, I get it!" Maggie said with a big, goofy grin. "You think I'm a pest! Just wait—I'm barely warmed up. I can be fifty times more annoying than this!"

"I don't doubt that for a minute," said Devon.

Maybe it was the stress of having to pick a bed. Whatever it was, I snapped. "Stop it! You two just met five seconds ago, and you already hate each other!" I yelled. Betsy was quietly sitting on the edge of her bottom bunk, watching all this.

Devon fluttered her eyelashes at me. "That's an overreaction."

Maggie nodded and shook her finger in my direction. "Temper, temper!"

The only thing more annoying than having my two best friends already arguing was the way they both always acted so cool and calm while I was losing it.

I took a deep breath. "Play nice, okay?" Maggie smiled sweetly and Devon shook her head and turned away. Betsy got busy making up her bottom bunk.

Once I lost my temper, it was always hard for me to

cool down again. I tried to distract myself by putting on my sheets and unpacking some stuff.

I dug out all my Converse high-tops in shades of aqua, purple, and orange, along with the red and yellow mates to the ones I had on my feet. Then I pulled out my final and favorite pair—my new see-through high-tops. I'd just bought them last weekend with some birthday money. They were waterproof, and the second I saw them, I had to have them. Wearing see-through sneakers would give me all kinds of new possibilities to make my socks a fashion statement. I lined all my shoes up under a bottom shelf by the wall.

Then I unpacked Melvin, my bear. I'd made him myself when I was seven at one of those workshops, and he had on red flannel pajamas and a matching nightcap.

Maggie grabbed him and hugged him. "Melvin, how ya been?" Then she propped him up against my pillow on my top bunk. I was glad she didn't seem too upset about the whole bunk bed thing.

When we heard the bell ringing, we all went to the dining hall for lunch. I explained to Devon that we'd sit at a table with our counselors and the other Cabin Four girls. Maggie and I kept seeing old friends from last year, and every time we stopped to talk to someone, Devon would yawn. It was like we were forcing her to listen to us recite the world capitals in reverse alphabetical order.

At lunch we got to meet the rest of the Side B girls. Kayla we'd already met in the cabin. She was pretty and slender, and there was something really graceful about the way she walked, like a ballet dancer. She had short hair and she was African American. The other new girl on Side B was Shelby Parsons, a really skinny girl with long bangs that almost hid her eyes. Boo Bauer I sort of knew from last summer. Every time Laurel-Ann went off on some long-winded discussion, Boo would lean over and say, "Hyphen-Ann, be careful you don't swallow your tongue."

Boo had blond hair and glasses, and she was a little on the chunky side. Even her name tag said "Boo" on it, so I wasn't sure what her real name was. She took one look at Shelby sitting next to her and said, "Here, have another taco. Or two, or three."

Shelby looked embarrassed. "I do eat. A lot. I just can't seem to gain weight."

"That's the same problem I have!" Boo insisted, which got a huge laugh.

I was just relieved to have other people around so that I didn't feel so torn between explaining things to Devon and catching up with Maggie.

Gloria Mendoza was the newbie counselor Laurel-Ann had groaned about, although I thought she looked nice enough, maybe a little on the shy side. She had dark brown hair and green eyes.

After lunch, there was rest hour, and while Gloria was getting to know her Side B campers, Wayward said we could do whatever we wanted. She covered her face with her cap and fell instantly asleep.

"How very Zen of her," Devon commented.

Betsy was busy unpacking. She dropped a little plastic case on the floor, and her top and bottom retainers bounced out and rolled under her bed. She had to crawl under her bunk to get them out. "Gross!" she moaned, holding the bottom one up. It had a dust bunny clinging to one of the wires.

"I'd sanitize that thoroughly if I were you," Devon advised.

When rest hour was over, I leaned down from my top bunk and smiled at Devon below me. "Now we go take our swim tests."

Her reaction was just as I expected. "I will not swim in that swamp you call a lake. I can only imagine what diseases I could catch."

Maggie let out a fake sneeze and scratched herself all over. "Jeez. Am I itchy! I think I'm getting some kind of weird rash. Oh, well. A dip in the lake will cool me down." I tried not to laugh. Maggie wasn't helping the situation at all.

After I'd gotten changed, I pulled my hair back, twisted it, and looped it into a loose knot. When I wanted my hair out of the way, I never bothered with clips or elastics. It was halfway down my back—wavy, thick, and dark—and usually I wore it down, except for swimming or sports.

I turned to Devon, who hadn't moved from her bunk. "Just come with us. It's really not that different from swimming in a pool."

"Sorry. I don't do lakes." She was reading and wouldn't even look up at me.

"Devon, everyone has to take the swim test the first day. It's required."

She lowered her book enough to make eye contact. "Required? So what happens if I don't take the swim test?"

"If you don't take the swim test, you can't go swimming. Or canoeing or kayaking. Basically, you can't go near the water. So you have to come," I explained. I stood there with my towel, waiting.

"Hmm," said Devon. "No test—I can't go near the water. Works for me."

CHAPTER 3

There was one good thing about Devon refusing to take her swim test. It gave Maggie and me a chance to talk by ourselves for the first time all summer as we walked down the hill to the lake.

"Chris, where did you dig up that Ghosty Girl, and why don't you bury her back in the grave you found her in?"

I squeezed my throbbing skull between my palms and growled. "Look, I know. She's making a horrible first impression. She's not like this at school. She's just not the outdoorsy type."

Betsy was walking with us, and she smiled in a friendly way and listened to our conversation, but otherwise, she kept quiet.

"Why did she come to summer camp? She'll be spending the whole month outdoors."

"I know. Well, this wasn't her idea." I told Maggie about how Devon was here against her will, and that she was mad she was missing out on a trip to Italy.

"I'd pick camp over Italy any old day. What's up with her, anyway? She acts like she's forty-five years old. When you said a friend was coming with you this year, I didn't expect anyone like that."

It was hard for me to explain everything to Maggie. Devon and I got to be friends in third grade when we both got put in the gifted program. We'd always compete to see who got the highest test scores. I'd usually beat Devon by a few points in math, but she'd win in vocabulary. We loved having these amazing debates about controversial topics. But most of all, we made each other laugh.

I knew Maggie wasn't exactly the intellectual type, but we still had lots in common. We liked to do all the adventurous stuff Pine Haven offered—rock climbing, rappelling, canoeing, or hiking. I was just the opposite of Devon when it came to any kind of outdoor activity. I loved it all.

"I just wish you could see the Devon I know," I told Maggie. "If she would get over being mad about being here, maybe she'll lighten up. She's funny and smart, and she's my best friend from school. And since you're my best friend from camp, I was hoping the two of you would be friends."

"I'll try to buddy up with Ghosty Girl. For your sake, Chris."

Was it asking too much for Devon and Maggie to become friends just because they were both friends with me? Maybe. With her dark red curls, Maggie reminded me of a friendly Irish setter. She was playful and fun, like a big goofy dog. Devon, on the other hand, was like a sleek black cat who wanted to curl up on a high perch somewhere and not be bothered. If you annoyed her, she'd hiss at you and show her claws.

I noticed that Betsy had slowly drifted away from Maggie and me as we'd been walking down the hill, and she'd caught up with Kayla, Shelby, and Laurel-Ann. I felt bad that we'd accidentally ignored her.

Practically everyone in camp was heading toward the lake, dressed in swimsuits and carrying towels, but campers were still arriving in cars, and we stopped to help a couple of parents who were wandering around with that lost look in their eyes.

When we finally got to the lake, we realized we were

going to have a long wait, because crowds of girls were already lined up in small groups, ready to take their swim tests. The swim staff was busy running around with clipboards and getting everyone organized.

Maggie and I didn't really care, though, because it gave us a chance to talk to some more of our old friends. It was nice not to have Devon standing next to me, yawning, but I didn't want her to feel like I'd deserted her.

Maggie and I saw Jordan Abernathy and Molly Chapman in a group sitting on a rock. "You're in Wayward's cabin, aren't you?" Molly called to us. "You're so lucky!" They were both really into horseback riding, which was Wayward's activity.

Whitney Carrington, a prissy girl I could hardly stand, walked up to us. "Something horrible just happened. Someone almost drowned. Alex Coleman, the swimming counselor, saved her life."

"Oh, darn! We missed all the fun!" moaned Maggie.

"I doubt anyone came close to drowning," I told her.

"Well, this new girl started swimming, but then she got tired, so Alex had to pull her out," Whitney insisted.

"Can Devon swim?" asked Maggie.

"Of course," I said. "She's not avoiding the lake for that reason."

"Oh my gosh," said Maggie. "Speak of the devil. Or should I say . . . Devon?"

Because to our complete surprise, Devon was walking toward us, wearing a black bikini and her flip-flops with the chunky soles that made her look three inches taller than she really was. When she saw us, she held up her hand like she was stopping traffic.

"Don't ask. I'm here against my will."

"What happened?" I asked. It made me so happy to see her. I didn't want her sitting in the cabin all alone, bored to death on the first day.

"Well, after everybody left the hovel, some lady in a skirt came by and saw I was all alone. She started giving me the third degree in the nicest way—'Are you afraid of the water, sweetheart? Can you swim, dear?' She seemed to think there was some dark reason I refused to swim in a swamp."

"It's not a swamp," said Maggie. "And did you remember to dunk yourself in sunscreen?"

Devon glanced sideways at Maggie and then back at me. "I could tell she was really concerned I might be some kind of outcast or something, so I told her I'd come take this ridiculous test."

"That was Eda, the director." I was so grateful she'd gotten Devon to take the test. Eda was probably the one person in camp who could have persuaded her.

"I promise you, the lake really isn't that bad." I hoped that the hundreds of little tadpoles that lived in the lake would stay deep in the water, out of sight. "You've still got mascara on," I told her.

Devon shrugged. "It's waterproof. But it doesn't matter. I'm not putting my head under."

Devon's "waterproof" comment made me laugh. It cracked me up that her main concern before the swim test was how well her mascara would hold up.

When it was our group's turn to go, Maggie did a cannonball off the end of the dock, and Devon went to the ladder and lowered herself carefully into the water, inch by inch.

"This swamp water is freezing!" she kept yelling. Then, after treading water with the rest of us for five minutes, she did a perfect breaststroke to the other side of the lake, making sure her head never went under.

But at least she'd done it.

CHAPTER 4

Monday, June 16

"My job's trash, Betsy has shelves, Chris has a free, and Devon—Devon's got the best job of all. Sweeping!" Maggie turned around from the job chart taped to the wall and grinned evilly at Devon, who was still in bed.

Devon sat up. "Since you're wearing dust mops, why don't you sweep?"

Maggie looked down at her furry black socks. I'd never seen anything like them—they were covered in this long, thick fur that made her look like she had gorilla feet. "Nah, don't want to get them dirty. Here you go, Cinderella." She took the broom and dustpan over to Devon's bed and laid them on top of her blankets. Devon kicked them off, and they fell on the floor with a clatter.

"Oh my gosh, it's freezing!" I said as I climbed out of

bed. With all the screens in the cabin, there was nothing to keep the cool air out and the warmth in. I'd almost forgotten what mornings in the mountains were like. I dug through my duffel for something warm to put on.

Wayward was still in bed. Usually counselors were the first ones up after the rising bell rang, but Wayward didn't look too motivated. Over on Side B, Gloria was up and trying to listen to Laurel-Ann's nonstop chatter while helping Kayla and Shelby figure out the jobs they had. I heard Boo tell Laurel-Ann her job was to follow a vow of silence for the rest of the week.

Devon got up and put her robe on. Then she took a towel, a bar of soap, and her shampoo from her shelf and started toward the door.

"Devon, where are you going?" I asked.

"To the showers. There better not be a line. Are you coming?"

I pulled on jeans and a tie-dyed shirt and then grabbed my red hoodie. I was so cold I even zipped it and pulled the hood up over my head. "You can't take a shower now. We've got to get the cabin ready for inspection," I said, wriggling my feet into one aqua and one orange high-top and bending down to tie them.

"What kind of inspection?"

"All the cabins get inspected after breakfast. You've

got to make your bed and do your job so the cabin's all clean and everything." As nice as it was for me to have a free pass, which meant I didn't have a job today, I almost wished Devon's name had landed on it this morning.

"And if there's anything wrong, like an unmade bed or dirt all over the floor because *someone* did a crappy job sweeping"—Maggie slid around on the wood floor in her gorilla socks—"then the whole cabin gets demerits. So start sweeping, Cindy."

Devon let out a disgusted grunt. "This is a nightmare. I fell asleep at summer camp and woke up drafted into the army. Can I at least take a shower first?"

"Not now. There's just not enough time. Nobody takes a shower before breakfast. You can take one later." I could already feel my patience evaporating. If Devon didn't watch it, she'd turn me into the Hulk before we even got through breakfast.

"You don't need to take a shower. You took one yesterday," Maggie said.

"News flash, Beefaroni. Some people with good hygiene habits shower every single day. But then, you're part gorilla, so why would you know that?"

Yesterday after the swim test, Devon had gone straight to the showers. She'd screamed when she saw a cricket near the drain of her shower stall, but eventually she got up the nerve to go inside. "I've seen nicer showers in third-world countries," she'd commented afterward.

"What does 'shelves' mean?" asked Betsy, smoothing her short blond hair down with both hands. While we were busy yakking, she'd already gotten dressed and made up her bed.

Wayward stretched and propped herself up on her pillow. "Shelves. Just . . . whatever. Make 'em look good, but don't sweat it. A few demerits never killed anyone."

Betsy popped out her retainers and put them in their little plastic case, then stood there looking around, not sure what to do with Wayward's vague directions.

"Okay, since I don't have a job, I'll help you all with yours," I told Devon and Betsy. Straightening the shelves was pretty easy; we weren't supposed to have wet towels or swimsuits hanging around on the hooks, and stuff needed to be fairly neat.

Then I held the dustpan for Devon while she swept. I was glad that she did her job like everyone else and didn't complain about it too much, but she muttered *el helado* a few times. One of these days, I'd tell her that word meant "ice cream."

After Devon finished sweeping, she got dressed and took her hair-straightening iron off the shelf by her bed.

"Where should I plug this in?"

Maggie, who'd just come back from emptying the trash cans, walked up and tapped the end of Devon's nose. "How about right here?"

Devon swatted Maggie's hand away and pointed the hair straightener at her like a weapon. "Back off, King Kong."

"You can't use hair straighteners in the cabin," I told her. "There aren't any outlets." Standing on my tip toes to make my bed, I smoothed out my blanket and propped Melvin up on my pillow. Besides, you don't have to iron your hair every day."

Devon wore her hair in a short, blunt cut, and it was already pretty straight, but she was really fussy about it being styled just the way she wanted it. She'd tried half a dozen times to get me to use her hair straightener, but I wouldn't let her near me with that thing. I'd keep my long, wavy locks just the way they were, thank you. I never even ironed my clothes. Why would I iron my hair?

"Great. No electricity. No running water. I think this hovel should have a 'Condemned' sign on it. Aren't there laws against making people live in substandard housing?"

I turned my back to her so she couldn't see my smile.

She knew she could always get a laugh out of me with her sarcastic comments, but I didn't want to encourage her at the moment.

"Anything else I should do?" asked Betsy.

"Nope, you're good," I told her. "Now we just go to breakfast." She was so agreeable. I wondered what she thought about me and my warring friends.

"Hurry up, Palechild. You're going to make us all late." Maggie stood in the doorway, swinging the screen door open and closed.

"Why don't you rush on down to the chow hall and tie on your feed bag?" Devon shot back. "I hope they're serving bananas."

We finished making Devon's bed, and it looked fairly presentable. She stopped in front of the little square mirror nailed to the wall. "I don't have any makeup on."

"Nobody wears makeup at camp!" Maggie let out a bellow from the doorway.

"Devon, you look fine. Let's go or we'll be late for breakfast." I ran a brush through my hair a couple of times and then tossed it on the shelf next to my top bunk.

I hoped every morning wouldn't be this stressful. I probably should've warned Devon last night about what the morning schedule was like. But then Betsy was new too, and she'd caught on pretty fast. Probably because she didn't have Devon's intense beauty regimen.

I did feel bad for Devon, though. I knew how out of place she was feeling at the moment. She never got on my nerves like this at home, so I made up my mind to help her get adjusted today.

For breakfast we had French toast, bacon, and fresh fruit. When Shelby handed Devon the plate of bacon, she passed it to Kayla. "No, thanks. I'm not a carnivore."

"Really? You're a vegetarian?" asked Betsy.

"Yes. I don't eat anything with a face." Devon piled sliced cantaloupe and strawberries on her plate. Then she reached for a little box of cold cereal.

"Hey, that's pretty cool. I've always admired vegetarians." Maggie nodded with what looked like sincere approval. "You know, choosing not to eat animals because there's so much other stuff you could eat. Could you pass me the fried pig flesh, please?" she asked, taking three slices when Boo handed her the plate.

Devon fluttered her eyelashes but didn't say a word.

After breakfast, Devon had hoped for a chance to shower and finish grooming. But we had bad news for her. We had to spend the rest of the morning at activities.

Maggie was looking over the activities list that was

taped up inside the cabin next to the morning job chart. "Ooh! Let's go to canoeing. If we pass enough progressions this week, we might be able to go on the first river trip."

That sounded great to me. I looked at Devon hopefully. "Do you want to try canoeing? It's a lot of fun."

She stared at me. "Have we met? How could you possibly think I'd want to paddle around a swamp in a leaky canoe?"

It was a good thing we weren't in a canoe right now, because she'd find herself suddenly swimming instead of boating. "Fine! What would you like to do?" I huffed.

"I'd like to lounge by the pool with a copy of *Vogue*. That's my idea of a vacation."

That was just the kind of thing Devon and I loved to do at home, so I felt horrible for getting annoyed at her. "That sounds good for later. During free time. We'll get our suits on, grab some towels and magazines, and go lay out by the lake. You won't even have to get wet. But for now, we have to go to activities," I told her.

"What happens if we don't?"

Maggie stood in front of the little square mirror, adjusting her Camp Crockett cap. "The counselors throw us in a cage full of rabid chipmunks."

"Wouldn't surprise me in the least."

I ignored them both. "Okay, these are our options: canoeing, riflery, tennis, crafts, or hiking," I read from the list. I looked at Devon. "Pick one."

Devon sighed heavily. "Crafts. I suppose that wouldn't be too torturous."

Maggie made a snorting sound. "Crafts? No way! Crafts is totally lame. I'm not going to crafts."

"Don't say that around Gloria. It's not her fault she's new and she got stuck being the crafts counselor," I reminded her.

"So? She's not even in the cabin now. All you do in crafts is make lanyards."

"What's a lanyard?" asked Devon.

"Look, it's Devon's first day. Let's let her pick the activities she wants to go to this morning. Then in the afternoon you can pick."

"Thanks, Mommy!" Maggie hugged me. "But when do you get to pick?"

I could feel my face getting hot with anger. "I really don't care what we do, as long as we're having fun. Okay? Let's try to have fun today!"

"Yippee," said Devon. "I can hardly wait."

"Cheer up, Ghosty Girl! Let's all three be happy campers."

Devon held up three fingers. "Read between the lines."

Maggie grinned sweetly. "Nice manicure."

"Let's go!" I snarled.

So on that note, my two best friends and I left for the Crafts Cabin.

It'll get easier, I told myself. Not every day could be this much work.

CHAPTER 5

But it didn't. At least crafts wasn't absolutely miserable. We made plates out of some kind of clay and painted designs on them. Then it was time to pick another activity. Surprisingly, Devon chose tennis. I'd never known her to play tennis before, but I was glad she was willing to try something new.

Tisdale, one of the tennis counselors, helped Devon and some of the other beginners work on backhands and forehands. Maggie and I took an empty court and started a match. Things were actually going fairly smoothly until Tisdale suggested that the girls she'd been working with try rallying with each other for a while.

"I'm supposed to practice the strokes I just learned," Devon announced, walking right out onto our court in the middle of Maggie's serve. Of course, I missed the return.

I ran to the corner of the court and scooped up the ball I'd missed.

"Off the court, Ghosty Girl! Chris and I are playing a match!" Maggie yelled from her side of the net.

Devon didn't even blink. There might as well have been a brick wall between Maggie and me instead of a net. "You want to play for a while? I think I could get the hang of this game with a little practice." Devon swung her racket back and forth in a few practice strokes.

Maggie ran up to the net. "Are you deaf? We're playing here, and you interrupted!"

Devon had this amazing gift for ignoring people when they got on her nerves. She walked right past Maggie to the other side of the court. Then she called to me, "Okay, ready when you are. But go easy on me to start." She gripped her racket in both hands, using the ready position that Tisdale had just showed her and the other beginners.

Maggie and I stood by the net. Her mouth fell open. "Palechild's got some nerve! She just barged right into the middle of our match!"

When I glanced at the other courts, I could see that everybody else was already paired up in doubles or singles groups. Tisdale was watching them and calling out reminders to follow through on their strokes. Now what was I supposed to do?

I turned to Maggie. "She doesn't have anyone else to play with, so let's just rally with her for a while. Then we'll finish our match."

As I walked over to Devon's side of the court, she glanced at me. "I thought we were going to play each other and let Beefaroni sit out for a while."

I hated this! Whatever I did to make Maggie happy annoyed Devon and vice versa. I felt like I should be sliced right down the middle.

"Devon, Maggie wants to play too. Look, three is an odd number in tennis. We don't have a fourth to play doubles. Want mc to sit down and you can rally with Maggie?"

"No, let's just do it the way you said—us two against what's-her-name over there."

"Serve!" I yelled to Maggie on the other side of the net.

Maggie served, all right. She hit every serve right to me instead of Devon, so I had no choice but to hit it back to her, and she kept the balls coming to me and me alone. It didn't take Devon long to catch on, and when she got bored and inspected her nails for a second, that was when Maggie decided to hit the ball right to her.

"Wake up, Palechild! I *thought* you wanted to play!"

"Not bad for a primate," Devon called across the net. "Does *National Geographic* know about the amazing tennis-playing gorilla? They could do a photo spread of you in the next issue."

This torture lasted for another twenty minutes until the bell rang. I've never been so relieved to have activities come to an end.

I had a slight break during lunch and rest hour, but then it was Maggie's turn to pick the afternoon activities, like I'd promised.

"Canoeing. I've been waiting all day for this. Let's go!" Maggie yelled. Betsy waved good-bye to us and left with Shelby.

Devon hadn't moved from where she lay on her bottom bunk, a copy of *Vogue* in front of her face. Most of our friends read *Seventeen*. I think Devon probably read that in preschool.

"*Vamos, chica.* Rest hour's over. Time for activities," I told her.

"You and King Kong go without me. I'm going to stay in the cabin and read."

Wayward was just waking up from her hour-long

nap, so I turned to her for support. "We have to go to activities, right, Wayward?"

Wayward smiled. "Whatever. Go to activities if you feel like it, Devon. Or you can chill in the cabin. Be Zen." She put on her sunglasses and plaid hat and walked out.

As cool as Wayward was, in some ways it might've been nice right at this moment to have a counselor who was a little more into the rules.

"Come on, Devon. You have to come with us."

Devon wouldn't even lower her magazine to look at me. "Right. Or I'll get thrown into a cage full of rabid chipmunks. Actually, I'd rather be eaten by chipmunks than spend the afternoon in a leaky canoe."

"Okay! See ya later," said Maggie cheerfully.

"Devon, Maggie went to all the activities you picked this morning. The least you can do is go to canoeing." I stood planted beside the bunk beds, determined not to move until she did.

"Fine, whatever. I'll go. But I'm not going to like it."

We were out the door and halfway to the lake when I noticed she had her magazine tucked under her arm. "Are you kidding me? You brought your copy of *Vogue* along?"

"Of course. I need *something* to entertain myself."

"You do realize we'll be in canoes, right, and not on a cruise ship?" I asked her.

"Don't remind me."

At the lake, all the canoes were lined up by the edge of the water. Michelle Burns, the perky canoeing counselor with curly blond hair, was going over terminology with a group of girls.

"Port is the left side, starboard is right. These are the gunwales"—she pointed to the canoe's side—"and the front is the bow and the back is the stern." Then she demonstrated a few strokes before we got out on the water. Maggie and I had canoed some last summer, so we already knew the basics.

"When's the first river trip?" asked Maggie.

"Next Monday. Interested in going?" Michelle asked with a grin.

"Definitely!" said Maggie.

"Not," added Devon.

Then Michelle said we could get into canoes and try out what we'd learned. Typically, there would be two people to a canoe, but as usual, the three of us had to stick together.

"I'm in the stern," Maggie called, wading out into the lake a little ways and climbing into the back of a canoe. I got in and sat in front of her.

Devon stood on the grassy edge of the lake and raised one eyebrow. "How am I supposed to get in?"

"What do you mean, how are you supposed to get in? Wade out and climb in!" Maggie yelled impatiently.

We were a foot or two away from the shore. Devon seemed to expect us to push the canoe all the way up on dry land and let her step right in.

"Wade in? I'm not going to *wade in*. These shoes are new."

I looked down and saw that Devon had on a new pair of canvas shoes with black laces that were so dazzlingly white I practically had to squint to look at them.

"You could take them off," I pointed out. I'd changed into my new clear, waterproof high-tops, and Maggie had on Crocs, so we'd been able to wade in, no problem.

"I refuse to take my shoes off. You scoot to the middle and let me climb in the front," Devon suggested.

"Whatever! Just so long as we do this sometime today," I growled. Already Meredith Orr and a new girl named Patty Nguyen were in the water and halfway across the lake.

Maggie swung the canoe around so the bow was pointed toward Devon, and I moved carefully to the middle, the canoe rocking slightly from the movement.

Then Maggie paddled forward so that the bow was

right up against the lake edge. Now Devon could literally step right in without getting wet. Maggie stuck her paddle down into the muddy lake bottom and held it to keep us from drifting while Devon climbed into the bow.

Once Devon had a seat, Maggie moved us away from the shore. I slid my paddle forward in the canoe so Devon could reach it.

"If you're sitting in the bow, you'll have to paddle," I told her.

Devon didn't touch the paddle. Instead she sat perched on the canoe seat, thumbing through her magazine, while Maggie was busy paddling with all her strength in the stern.

"Devon, you have to paddle!" I yelled. "Stop reading and help out!"

"Yeah, Ghosty Girl. I'm doing all the work here," Maggie called from the stern. She swung her paddle forward and flicked the blade up so that droplets of water hit the back of Devon's shirt. "Come on, let's see some arm muscle."

Devon flinched a little when the water drops hit her, but she didn't turn around. "If I feel another drop of water on me, you'll be flossing your teeth with that paddle," she said coolly.

"Oh, yeah?" Maggie yelled. "How about I feed your magazine to the fishies?"

I clutched my head between my palms, and a low rumbling sound came out of my throat, kind of like the one my cat Gitana would make just before coughing up a hair ball. It was a warning sound that meant some bad eruption was about to happen.

"*¡Me vuelvo loca!* I mean it! You two are this close to driving me completely insane!"

"Hey, Chris—you know what we forgot to do? A dunk test!" Maggie yelled.

She scooted beside me in the middle and was getting into position to flip the canoe over. Her hands gripped the gunwales of the starboard side while her feet pushed down with a huge thrust on the port side. The whole canoe tipped dangerously sideways.

Hey! *Was water coming in?* She was going to . . .

"Maggie, don't—"

I grabbed the starboard gunwales to keep from falling, but I was losing my balance and felt myself falling backward. I sucked in air just before I hit the water. My ears were muffled, my eyes shut instinctively, and the icy, wet chill flooding over me made every muscle in my body tense. A tidal wave came crashing over my head as the canoe flipped. I coughed and sputtered, trying to catch my breath.

At the same second I'd hit the water, I'd felt two giant splashes on either side of me. My confused brain registered that Devon and Maggie had just gone under too.

As soon as my head was above water I opened my eyes. "Grab"—I coughed, trying to catch my breath—"grab the canoe!" My hair hung in my eyes and I pushed it out of the way, then lunged forward till I reached the overturned canoe.

"I didn't mean to! I swear! I didn't mean to!" Maggie was yelling to the right of me. A wet form on my left was pawing at the overturned canoe, trying to find a place to hold on.

The sides of a canoe are curved, so it's not exactly the easiest object to grab onto when you've just been dumped unexpectedly out of it. But I managed to get my upper body out of the water enough so that I could cling to the edge. Then I was able to hang on and look around.

Devon was on my left, Maggie on my right, both of them clinging to the overturned canoe like I was. All of us were still gasping for breath. Devon's face was hidden by a black mask of wet hair. Maggie held on to the canoe with one arm and reached for her

Camp Crockett cap floating nearby with the other.

"I'm so sorry! It was a total accident! I just . . . ," Maggie said in a choked voice.

"Forget about it! We've got to flip this over!" I shouted.

I could hear Michelle calling out instructions to us, but I couldn't tell what she was saying. "Need any help?" asked Meredith and Patty, approaching us in their canoe.

"I think we're okay!" I called back to them.

At least Maggie and I had done a dunk test last summer, so we knew the only way to turn the canoe over would be to flip it toward us.

"Devon, help! We've got to grab it this way!" I told her. When she saw what Maggie and I were doing, she grabbed the edge of the canoe, and after a few minutes of desperate splashing, the three of us managed to flip it upright again. Then we all had to try to climb into it without tipping it over again.

Once we were back in, I saw that one paddle had stayed in the canoe, tucked under the seat, and the other was floating a few feet away. Meredith reached out and grabbed it, then paddled close enough to hand it to us.

The canoe was about half-full of water but still floating, so we started paddling. Meredith and Patty backed out of our way.

"I honestly didn't mean to dunk us!" Maggie wailed. "I was just playing around. All I wanted to do was rock the boat a little, but then . . . I don't know what happened!"

"Let's just get to the shore," I told her. Devon hadn't said a word.

I remembered turning around to see what Maggie was up to and losing my balance. When I'd grabbed the gunwales, I might have actually helped Maggie flip us. It probably *had* been an accident. And from the way her voice sounded, I could tell she was really upset. The joke had backfired on her, and we'd all paid the price.

When we'd made it to shallow water, Maggie jumped out and pulled our waterlogged canoe in the rest of the way. Then Devon and I climbed out.

"I never said we were doing dunk tests today," said Michelle, a hint of annoyance in her voice. She waded out to help Maggie pull the canoe in. "But now that you've dunked it, help me empty the water out."

The dunk test actually was a skill we'd have to learn at some point—take the canoe out, intentionally flip it, and then get back in and paddle to shore, usually with a boatful of water. If you wanted to go on a river trip, you had to demonstrate to the canoeing staff that you could handle an emergency situation.

"I guess we passed this progression at least, right?" Maggie asked with an embarrassed smile.

Maggie and I helped Michelle lift the canoe up and over enough so that the water started pouring out over the gunwales. Devon stood dripping on the bank and watched us silently.

Meredith and Patty paddled up in their canoe. They'd managed to grab Devon's magazine, which had stayed afloat on the surface of the water during our whole cap-sizing adventure.

Maggie took the soggy mass of wet paper from Patty's outstretched hand. She walked up to Devon and handed her the ruined magazine. "Devon . . . what can I say? I'm an idiot sometimes. I swear on a stack of Bibles ten feet high—I didn't mean to turn us over out there."

Devon's black hair was plastered around her face. She dropped the magazine on the ground and stood with her arms crossed, shivering slightly in her wet clothes. Then she looked directly at me. "I think you have a decision to make."

"What are you talking about?" I asked, twisting my wet hair to wring some of the water out of it. Next to me, Maggie was shaking herself like a dog who'd just escaped from an unexpected bath.

"I refuse to spend another second with this ape you call a friend. You can be her best friend or you can be my best friend, but not both." Devon leveled her eyes at me.

"Make your decision."

CHAPTER 6

"You can't do this to me! You can't make me choose between you!"

Devon was lying on her bottom bunk, propped up on her pillow, dry now, with a copy of *Brave New World* in front of her face. Apparently, she'd brought enough reading material to last her through another six or seven canoeing accidents.

Maggie sat on her top bunk, her legs dangling over the side. She was wearing her black gorilla socks. The water had been freezing cold, and we had all wanted to get warm and dry as fast as we could.

Our wet clothes were hanging up to dry. Devon's new shoes were next to my clear high-tops and Maggie's Crocs. They'd dry out eventually, but they'd probably never have that bright white look again.

It hadn't been much fun for me to fall out of a canoe, but I really felt awful about Devon getting dunked. I knew how she hated doing outdoorsy things. Now she'd fallen into the "swamp," ruined her magazine, and waterlogged her brand-new shoes. She had every right to be furious with Maggie.

Maggie kicked her legs against the bunk rail. "Hey, Devon, this is really stressing Chris out. You and I should try to get along."

I think that might've been the first time I'd ever heard Maggie actually call Devon by her real name. But Devon wouldn't look up from her book. She was an ice princess when she got mad—absolutely cold. And very calm. I was just the opposite. In some ways, I kind of wished I could stay calm like that when I got mad instead of spewing out hot lava like Mount Kilauea.

Maggie picked up her pillow and punched it with her fist. "I'm really, really sorry. I swear, though, I was just fooling around. I just meant to rock the canoe and shake you up a bit to get a few laughs."

Devon didn't even bat an eyelash.

"But it's hard to laugh with your lungs full of lake water. I take full responsibility for this whole mess."

I had to admire the way Maggie admitted it was her fault. I hated admitting I was wrong about anything. I don't know why—I've just never been very good at apologizing to people or taking the blame for stuff.

I believed Maggie when she said she hadn't meant to dump us all out. All the way back to the cabin, I'd yelled at her for pulling such a stupid stunt. She walked along with her shoulders slumped and her rusty curls hanging in limp little ringlets all over her head. "I'm an idiot! I'm sorry!" she kept saying. I think it really was an accident.

Clutching her pillow, Maggie climbed down from her top bunk and went over to Devon. "Here, beat me over the head with this a few times. I deserve it, and it'll make you feel better." She bent her head down to make it an easy target.

Devon lowered her book and looked past Maggie at me. "I refuse to spend another minute with this creature. It's absolutely impossible that the two of us could ever be friends."

"Don't you think 'impossible' is a pretty strong word? I'm not asking you two to become best friends, but can't you . . . maybe try to put up with each other?" I asked.

"It's not going to happen," Devon said coolly.

"Why? You're both still getting to know each other. And . . . maybe you're both a little jealous of each other," I suggested.

Devon flipped her eyes upward. Her hair was still wet, and the ends were curling up. I bet it was driving her crazy, not being able to use her straightener on it. "Me jealous? Of Gorilla Feet there? How could I possibly be jealous of her? She's stupid and annoying."

"Hey, stop! That's harsh. You don't have to get mean about it," I told her.

Devon tossed her book aside and sat up. "She's an absolute *calcetines*."

I kept a straight face and made a mental note to tell Maggie later that Devon had called her a pair of socks.

Usually Maggie would've had some funny comeback for an insult like that, but she kept quiet. She dropped her pillow and slouched over to her trunk, where she sat down with her chin in her hands, looking pretty depressed.

"Devon, Maggie is not stupid. You two just have completely different personalities."

"Exactly. Which is why we can never be friends."

"Well, I'm not going to choose between you, so you can forget that!" I informed her.

Maybe I had been wrong to think that the two of

them could get along. They *were* so completely different. Devon had been a total pain from the moment we got on the bus to come here, but I still couldn't dump her. It wasn't all her fault for hating camp so much, and I could see how someone like Maggie could get on her nerves. Irish setters usually did rub black cats the wrong way.

But I wasn't about to give up what could be a fun summer with Maggie just because Devon hated every single thing about Pine Haven. If I could have it my way, I'd spend all my time at activities with Maggie, and then come back at the end of the day and hang out with Devon in the cabin and talk.

"Okay, I can see how maybe this won't work—the three of us spending all our time together," I said slowly, trying to figure out what I was going to say next. "But both of you are still my two best friends."

Devon sat on her bunk without moving a muscle, and Maggie stared absently at the wooden floor. Neither one of them said anything.

"So instead of the three of us doing everything together . . . maybe I could split my time evenly between both of you."

"That doesn't seem fair to you," said Maggie.

"Well, I don't know what else to do." Once again, I was wishing for a coin to toss so I could make a fair decision. Glancing around the cabin for something, I noticed Melvin propped up on my pillow and went over and grabbed him by his furry foot.

"Okay, tomorrow morning for activities, I'll go with one of you. Then in the afternoon, I'll go with the other. If Melvin lands faceup, I'll go with Devon in the morning. Facedown, I'll go with Maggie."

"I would get the butt end of the deal," Maggie observed.

I tossed Melvin in the air as high as the rafters and he came down, landing on the floor at my feet. But he was lying on his side.

I huffed in exasperation. "That didn't count. I'll do it again."

"Don't bother," said Devon, snatching up Melvin by the paw before I could reach him. She smashed his bear face into the floor. The three of us sat there, looking at Melvin lying on his stomach, his furry tail sticking out of the slit of his red flannel pajama bottoms.

"There," said Devon firmly. "The decision's been made. You can spend all day tomorrow with Beefaroni for all I care."

CHAPTER 7

Wednesday, June 18

"Happy birthday to you! Happy birthday to you! Happy birthday, dear Chris! Happy birthday to you!" sang all my cabinmates with a huge amount of energy. Birthdays at camp always got a lot of attention.

"Thanks, everybody!" I said.

It was the end of lunch, and the CATs had just come out of the kitchen carrying a birthday cake lit up with twelve candles. Everyone in the dining hall was watching.

I smiled and could feel myself blushing a little from being the center of attention. I closed my eyes and made my wish. *I want to stay friends with Devon and Maggie, and I want to do it without both of them driving me loca!* Then I opened my eyes, and the whole dining hall clapped and cheered as I blew out all the candles in one breath.

That was a good omen. Now my wish would come true.

My cabinmates had been thrilled when they'd found out it was my birthday. Our whole cabin got to eat birthday cake and ice cream for dessert while the rest of the dining hall was having strawberry Jell-O.

"So . . . June. What sign are you? I'm Leo, by the way. The lion. Don't you think all the horoscope stuff is fascinating? I do," said Laurel-Ann while Gloria was busy cutting the cake.

"I'm Gemini. The twins," I told her. "We're supposed to have two sides to our personalities." Gloria handed me the first slice. It was chocolate cake with white frosting. My favorite was yellow cake with chocolate frosting, but at least I had cake on my birthday.

"Oh, that explains a lot!" Betsy said with a laugh.

"What's that supposed to mean?" I asked around a mouthful of cake.

"Well, it explains how you could be friends with Maggie and Devon at the same time," she said.

Everybody at the table laughed. Devon fluttered her eyelashes, and Maggie opened her mouth to show Devon her half-eaten birthday cake.

I'd never really thought of that as an explanation

for why I had two such different best friends. Did I have a split personality? All I knew was that I liked both of them for different reasons. Some other things about me seemed two-sided. Like, I was totally into American culture, but I loved my Puerto Rican heritage too. And I was sort of a tomboy who liked outdoor adventures, but I liked girl stuff, too, like dressing up for special occasions.

"Do you mind having your birthday away from your family?" asked Kayla.

"Not too much. My family celebrated with me last Saturday. So in a way, it's like having two birthdays."

On Saturday we'd had *pasteles*, which was my favorite Puerto Rican dish: spicy meat wrapped in plantain leaves. We always had them around the holidays, and that was also the dish I wanted for my birthday dinner.

"Anybody famous born on your birthday?" asked Boo.

"Well, Paul McCartney, that old Beatles guy, and some other people I've never heard of."

"He's a vegetarian. His wife Linda even wrote vegetarian cookbooks," Devon pointed out. She'd eaten a bean-and-rice burrito for lunch. Pine Haven's cooks always made sure there was some kind of veggie dish at every meal.

"I've thought about becoming a vegetarian," said

Maggie. "But I'd miss hamburgers and fried chicken. And I love slabs of fried pig flesh for breakfast." She stuffed a giant forkful of cake into her mouth, licking her lips to catch a stray bit of frosting.

Betsy covered her face with her hands. "Maggie, you're really starting to turn me off bacon."

After lunch, I got to check my mail, and I was really happy to see that my little cubby on the dining hall porch was stuffed with cards and e-mail printouts, all wishing me happy birthday and *feliz cumpleaños*. That morning I'd gotten to go to the office and call my parents. You only got to call home for birthdays and emergencies.

Back at the cabin, Devon solemnly handed me a package wrapped in brown paper towels from Solitary. "I know this is exactly what you wanted."

I laughed when I unwrapped it. It was the plate she'd painted in crafts.

"Gee, thanks," I told her. "Now I've got two."

"Thanks for not snubbing my handmade gift," said Devon. "Maybe the next time I go to crafts I can knit you a new pair of high-tops."

When Maggie saw that, she grabbed the plate she'd made from her shelf and tossed it to me like a Frisbee. Luckily, I caught it. "Here ya go, Kachina. Happy birthday. And congratulations. It's triplets."

"See. You two have the same taste in gifts," I pointed out.

Betsy smiled when I said that. I could tell she was aware of all the ups and downs I was having with Devon and Maggie.

Like yesterday. Devon absolutely insisted that I go to every activity with Maggie. "The bear has spoken, Chris," she said anytime I tried to suggest that I could split the day up between her and Maggie.

So Maggie and I *had* spent the day together, but I worried about Devon the whole time. Was she secretly mad at me and just acting like she didn't care? I knew I couldn't let this go on much longer—the two of us not hanging out together at all. It might really damage our friendship.

So after rest hour was over, everyone was leaving for activities. I climbed down from my top bunk and peeked through the metal rails at Devon lying on her bottom bunk.

"I want you to give me another birthday present," I told her.

Devon raised her eyebrows at me. "Sorry, I'm miles from the nearest mall, so a lousy handmade plate is all I can do for you right now."

"I'm serious. This is something I really want. Go

to activities with me this afternoon. Just you and me." I'd really missed having her around yesterday, cracking jokes and making me laugh.

"What about the banana eater? Won't she be lonely?" Devon asked with a frown.

"The banana eater and I spent all morning together at canoeing. Now I want to hang out with you for the rest of the day."

Devon sighed and didn't say anything. She wouldn't look at me either. Maybe she really was kind of mad at me for having another best friend besides her.

"You have to, Devon! It's my birthday, so I get whatever I want for the whole day," I told her firmly.

Maggie was going on a hike with a big group to Frogmouth Rock. I'd planned on going with her, until I'd decided to spend the afternoon with Devon instead.

"Hey, Christina Kachina—I'll see you later, okay?" Maggie said.

"Okay, later, Windsoroni." I couldn't help feeling like I was deserting her, but I'd talked this over with her while we were canoeing this morning, and she'd agreed to it.

Devon perked up a little after Maggie was out of the cabin. "Let's go to archery," I suggested. "You haven't tried that yet. You might actually like it."

She yawned. "Oh, yeah? What are we hunting? Wild boars?"

"No, wild straw targets. They can be pretty ferocious too. Let's go."

It was a beautiful afternoon with big, fluffy white clouds sailing across the blue sky. I loved having a summer birthday. No school and an entire day of outdoor fun. What could be better?

The archery range was basically an open field with big, round, straw targets that had brightly colored rings of white, black, blue, red, and finally gold in the center.

We got our bows and arrows from Margaret White, the archery counselor. "I'll give Devon a quick demo," I told Margaret, so she could help some of the other newbies.

I showed Devon how you were supposed to straddle the white line spray-painted in the grass so that your body faced sideways. Then you turned only your head toward the target, with your chin lined up to your shoulder. That way you could hold the bow in one hand and pull the string all the way back to your ear with the other hand.

"The string feels really resistant at first, but you'll get used to it," I told Devon. We were using leather tabs to protect our fingers from getting blisters from the string.

"Your left arm should be straight and your right arm will be bent like this." I demonstrated. "Then, when you aim, point the arrow down slightly because it tends to fly up when you release it."

I took aim and hit in the blue ring. "Okay, go ahead and try it," I told Devon.

She'd been watching me carefully while I'd shot my first arrow, and now she followed my directions closely. She pulled the string back, took aim, and then released the arrow. It sailed through the air and struck the target with a thwacking sound. Devon's arrow had landed in the red, one ring closer to the center than mine.

"Excellent!" I shouted. "Look how great you did— and on your first try."

Devon lowered her bow and smiled slightly. Then she shot the rest of her arrows, hitting the target every single time. Nearby, Isabel Zeigler was shooting arrows that fell into the grass, two or three feet short of the target.

"See, you're a natural at this," I told her when everyone was finished shooting and we could retrieve our arrows.

Devon smiled, obviously pleased with her performance. "I feel like Diana, goddess of the hunt."

Last year in sixth grade, we'd spent a whole unit

of social studies studying mythology, and Devon and I had loved every minute of it. "Yeah, and archery has some real benefits. It makes your chest muscles stronger. We could go up a whole cup size!" I said with a laugh.

Devon smiled slyly. "Why aren't we coming here every day then?" she asked.

"We could. Definitely!" I loved the way we were laughing and having fun together, just like we always did back home.

"See, this is a good birthday present. This is just what I wanted. I was hoping you'd start to like some things about camp."

Devon grimaced when I said that. "Don't remind me. Every single day I think about what I'm missing. I mean, really, Chris—when will I ever get a chance to go to Europe again?"

We were back at the line, ready to shoot again. I positioned my arrow and tried to aim a little more carefully this time. It was a tiny bit annoying that Devon was beating me on her very first archery visit.

"Have you gotten a postcard or anything from your parents yet?" I asked.

"Not yet. I suppose it takes awhile for mail to get all the way across the Atlantic Ocean," she said with annoyance. She quickly aimed her arrow and shot, hitting right in the gold center.

"Good shot," I admitted. "Look, I know Pine Haven would've been your last choice of where to spend a month of summer vacation, but at least we're together. We can still have a good time like we always do, right?" I asked.

"We *could* have a good time if that gorilla wasn't in the way. Chris, I honestly have no idea what you see in her."

Devon's next shot hit in the red. So far she'd hit every single arrow in the inner three rings.

"Devon, don't start. You just don't get Maggie the way I do. And we like to do a lot of the same things."

I'd never go on any river trips, or take a hike, or even swim in the lake if I spent all my time with Devon.

"You'd *never* be friends with her back home," she went on. "First of all, there's no way she'd ever make it into the gifted program."

I had raised my bow and was about to take aim when I lowered it and glared at Devon. "She's not stupid. She happens to be a good friend of mine."

Devon had her back to me so she could take aim again. She shot all her arrows before she said anything else.

"What do the two of you do together? Blaze trails? Hunt grizzlies?"

"I think you're jealous, Devon," I said. "Can't you try to be a little more mature about this and accept the fact that I can have two best friends?"

Devon jabbed the point of her arrow into the grass, inches from my purple and yellow high-tops. It wavered back and forth a little from the force. "Mature? *Mature?* You're telling me to be mature? Have you seen the way *you* act around her? You two are like a couple of bratty kindergartners when you're together."

I knew I'd hit a sore spot with Devon, who took pride in the fact that she acted like she was in her midthirties. At least.

"Why? Because we know how to have fun? I made a point of spending the afternoon with you when I could be having a lot more fun with Maggie. I bet she's the life of the party on the hike she's on right now. Too bad I'm not with her."

As soon as I'd said that, I felt bad. But it was too late, I couldn't take it back. I noticed how Devon's lips pressed together when she heard it. She held her head up, trying to act like she didn't care about the mean thing I'd just said.

"Oh, I'm sure she is. I can see her now in the trees—

hanging upside down by her toes." Devon swatted at the end of the arrow stuck in the grass.

I felt so guilty. I really had been having fun with Devon. I should apologize now, tell her I didn't really mean that.

Instead I snatched her arrow out of the grass and brushed the dirt off its pointed tip, then nocked it into the bow string and aimed at the target. It stuck in the gold—my first shot to hit dead center since we'd started.

"Hey, that was my arrow," Devon protested.

"Too bad," I told her. "And you're ruining my birthday."

"I'm not ruining your birthday," she snapped.

She wasn't really. I didn't want us to fight. But I couldn't force an apology out of my mouth.

"Well . . . it started out happy but it's gotten worse as the day goes on," I said. "Thanks to you." I stood there, fuming. I knew I was just making things worse, but I couldn't seem to stop myself.

Devon laid her bow down in the grass and started to walk off. When she was about ten feet away, she glanced over her shoulder. "Cheer up. You can spend the rest of the day with your *best* friend. I'm sure you two will have more fun than a barrel of monkeys."

CHAPTER 8

Friday, June 20

"I think it's about to start pouring any second now," I predicted.

Maggie looked up at the dark sky. A layer of heavy gray clouds was hanging low overhead, and all around us was that still, expectant feeling just before a storm hit.

We were paddling around on the lake, working on our newest strokes. Besides Maggie and me, Meredith Orr and Patty Nguyen were a couple of other canoeing regulars. And Boo had started coming to canoeing a lot with her friend Abby Harper.

Michelle and Steve (the canoeing guide who went along on all the river trips) had said that if we passed the next two progressions, our little group would be able to go on the Monday river trip.

"Hey, everyone! Bring the canoes in now!" Michelle called from the edge of the lake. The activity period was only halfway over, so she must have been concerned about the way the sky looked.

Maggie and I paddled toward the shore.

"I wonder . . . ," I started to say.

"Wonder what?" Maggie asked, looking over her shoulder at me from the bow of the canoe.

"I wonder if we're about to get drenched," I said finally.

I'd been about to say *I wonder where Devon is right now*, but I'd stopped myself.

Devon and I didn't stay mad at each other on my birthday, luckily. Right before lights-out that night, I'd found a note on my pillow, underneath Melvin.

> Dear Chris,
> My sincerest apologies for "ruining" your birthday. It actually was somewhat entertaining to shoot arrows at ferocious straw targets. I can't explain why I got irritated like that.
> Could it be that I am the slightest bit jealous of that primate you call a friend? It seems impossible. After all, I've learned

to walk upright. I'll admit, the fact that she has attained the status of "best" friend with you does cause me a slight pain in my heart. Notice I said slight. We're not talking cardiac here. I guess it's that I always thought I held exclusive rights to that position myself.

I was the one who behaved like a bratty kindergartner today when I walked away. So I gave myself an appropriate punishment. I took a ten-minute time-out and I'm depriving myself of apple juice and animal crackers. So I hope you'll forgive me, because I'd hate to lose you as a friend.

Your Best Friend,

Devon (i.e., the Smart One, not to be confused with the Hairy One)

After I'd read her note, I couldn't stop laughing. That was exactly why we were friends in the first place—because of her amazing sense of humor.

It was a good thing Devon had apologized. Not that I didn't feel guilty about telling her I'd be having more fun with Maggie. I really did feel bad about that remark. But I've never been very good at apologies.

The only problem was, now I was back to trying to divide my time evenly between the two of them. Every time I was with Maggie, I wondered if Devon was lonely without me, and the whole time I was with Devon, I was thinking about what Maggie was doing. It was a constant juggling act, and I was spending all my energy trying to keep the black cat and the Irish setter in the air without dropping one of them.

"Hey! Hurry up—the rain's coming!" Michelle yelled at us, as we jumped out of the canoe and pulled it up on the shore. Boo and Abby had already brought their canoe in, and Meredith and Patty were right behind us.

We'd barely put our paddles away in the storage shed when the rain started coming down in sheets.

"Senior Lodge!" yelled Michelle. Everyone on the lake was running in that direction, because it was the closest form of shelter.

By the time we all made it to the lodge, we were absolutely drenched. There were about fifteen of us, and everyone was laughing and talking because we'd gotten so wet and now it was a major downpour outside.

Libby Sheppard and Alex Coleman, a couple of swimming counselors, found some matches on the fireplace mantel and started a fire. We all crowded around it to dry off and get warm.

"I love rainy days! I love them!" said Michelle, rubbing her hands through her curly blond hair and scattering water droplets on everyone around her.

I loved them too, only I wished Devon was here with us. In a big group like this, maybe she wouldn't mind being around Maggie. I wondered what she was doing now.

"So this is Senior Lodge," said Patty, looking up at the big wooden beams overhead. "I've never been in here."

Neither had I, come to think of it. The lodges were the places where we had evening programs and assemblies. Like ours, this lodge was built out of stone and had high ceilings. Both the front and back doors of the lodge were open, and so were all the windows. The windows didn't have any screens, so the smell of the rain and the smoke from the fire blended together.

"I wish we had some marshmallows," said Meredith. "We could roast them over the fire."

"Never mind marshmallows." Michelle grinned at everyone. "This is the perfect weather for ghost stories! Ever heard the story of the Ghost Dog?"

"Don't tell that one!" said Candice Rosenfeld, a Senior. "It's too sad."

"No, let her tell it," said Trish Morales. "Go ahead, Michelle."

"Okay, everyone. This is a true story. A young couple with a new baby had just moved into their dream house. Or so they thought. It was an old two-story brick home with a wide front porch and tall shade trees in the yard. But as soon as they moved in, they sensed an evil presence tormenting their baby."

Michelle went on in a low voice, telling about how the baby would always wake up screaming every time she was left alone in her crib. Their old German shepherd stayed in the room to guard the baby, but he would growl and pace the room with all the hair standing up on his back. The room would feel icy cold, even though it was the middle of a hot summer.

And then one time the baby was screaming in terror and the dog was barking uncontrollably at something, but as the couple ran to check on them, they heard a sharp bark, and then—silence. They found the old dog dead on the floor, the baby still whimpering in her crib.

Michelle paused, and we all sat there, not moving. I looked out the window at the gray clouds and the pounding rain and kind of wished we'd never started telling ghost stories in the first place.

Michelle went on, "One day they left the baby alone for a nap. A little while later they heard her shriek in terror. When they tried to get into the room, the door was locked! Inside, the baby kept screaming. Only this time, they heard an evil cackle coming from the room! The father threw his whole weight against the door, trying to break in, but it wouldn't budge.

"As they beat on the door, they heard ferocious barking inside, like a dog attacking. An otherworldly scream pierced the air and then . . . everything was quiet.

"The doorknob turned by itself, the door swung open, and the parents found the baby lying safe in her crib. She still had tears on her cheeks, but she was smiling up at them, and from that moment on, they never once felt the evil presence in their house again. The parents were convinced that the spirit of their faithful dog had protected their baby even after death."

Michelle was silent, looking around at all of us.

Maggie cleared her throat. "And that's a true story? How do you know?"

"How do I know? You know the baby in the story?" Michelle leaned forward, staring at Maggie with wide eyes. "That baby was me!"

Boo cupped her hands over her mouth and groaned, "Boo! Boo! That's so lame." Her glasses looked steamy from being out in the rain.

"Hey, stop booing Michelle," said Maggie. "Is that why we call you Boo?"

Her friend Abby jumped off the bench and laughed. "No way! Don't you all know what her real name is? Belinda!"

"Shut up, Abigail! No one asked you." Boo punched Abby in the arm. "Just kidding, Michelle. Good story."

"Let's sing something," suggested Libby Sheppard, because everyone had gotten really quiet listening to Michelle's story.

Pine Haven was really big on singing. Anytime we were in a group—at an assembly, on a trip, in the dining hall—we'd end up singing. Libby started off the first lines of "Light Up the Campfire," which had the same tune as "Down in the Valley."

Light up the campfire, sing us a song
Here at Pine Haven, we all belong
We all belong here, we all belong
Here at Pine Haven, we all belong.

When we first met, friend, we were both new
Strangers we were, friend, till I met you
Till I met you, friend, till I met you
Strangers we were, friend, till I met you.

Now we are sisters, happy are we
Here we are sisters, always we'll be
Sisters forever, always we'll be
Here we are sisters, always we'll be.

Since we were dry now, a bunch of us went out on the porch to really enjoy the downpour. Raindrops pelted the surface of the lake, sometimes hard and sometimes softer. I felt like I could sit on the porch all day and watch the rain come down.

Finally, late in the afternoon, it started to let up. As we left the lodge, big gray clouds still hung in the sky, and water dripped from all the tree branches. The rain made the air really cool, and Maggie, Boo, and I jumped over puddles as we ran down Middler Line to our cabin. We passed Reb Callison, Jennifer Lawrence, and a newbie named Kelly covered from head to toe in mud, laughing so hard they were falling over themselves.

Maggie gave her shirt a deep sniff. "I smell like wood smoke."

I sniffed mine, too. "Yeah, I love that smell."

Boo pushed open the cabin door, and we walked into the middle of a little crowd standing around on Side A: Shelby, Laurel-Ann, Kayla, and Devon.

Something was lying on Devon's bed. It looked like a bundle of laundry.

"What's up?" I asked. We were all looking at the thing. The bundle seemed to have a face. And hair. And it had a note pinned to it. I leaned over Devon's bed. "What is it?"

"Oh, that?" said Devon. "It's supposed to be me. Yours Truly. Someone created this little masterpiece and left it on my bed."

CHAPTER 9

Lying on Devon's bottom bunk was a white pillowcase stuffed full of something, probably clothes. On the front of the pillowcase, someone had drawn a face—two eyes with long eyelashes, two rosy cheeks, and a pink, pouting pair of lips. It looked like it'd been done with eyeliner, rouge, and lip gloss. There was a black cami pulled over the top of the pillowcase for hair. Around the "neck" of the pillowcase was the cord of Devon's hair straightener, hanging down like some weird necklace.

One of Devon's clean white T-shirts was spread out on the bed under the pillowcase head, along with a pair of black shorts. White socks had been stuffed and laid out for arms and legs.

"We've just discovered your body!" I said.

Maggie started laughing. "Jeez! Somebody sure got creative!"

"I have to hand it to you, Beefaroni," said Devon. "It's pretty amusing. Pretty clever. I didn't think you had it in you." Devon picked up the note pinned to her "body."

Then Betsy walked in and looked at all of us just standing there, staring at this stuffed pillowcase lying on Devon's bed. "Uh, I guess I missed something."

Devon sighed. "Okay. For the late arrivals: That's supposed to be me lying on the bed there. And here's what the note says."

Devon held up the paper and started reading very dramatically, with hand gestures.

"Devon's Top Ten Reasons for Hating Summer Camp:

10. I can't iron my hair every day.
9. I don't do swamps.
8. Too many pig-flesh eaters.
7. North Carolina looks nothing like Italy.
6. Everyone has a ridiculous nickname.
5. Those canoe paddles ruined my manacure.
4. Rabid chipmunks will probably attack soon.
3. Our hovel has a CONDEMNED sign on it.

2. I have a gorilla for a roommate.

1. When did I get drafted into the army?"

When she was finished, she took a deep bow. We all applauded and cheered. Everyone was laughing hysterically. The list by itself was funny enough, but with Devon reading it in her usual ultra-sarcastic tone, it was even better. At least she was being a good sport about this little prank. I doubted I would've reacted the same way if someone had done that to me.

"Oh my gosh! Who wrote that? This is a crack-up," said Shelby.

"I don't have a ridiculous nickname!" Betsy protested. "I'm the only one on Side A who doesn't have a nickname. Someone want to give me one?" she asked over all the laughing.

"That really is funny," said Boo, pushing her glasses up her nose and bending down to inspect the face on the pillowcase. "I'd recognize you anywhere."

"Thank you. I'm glad you all find my misery so amusing." Devon handed the note to Maggie. "You misspelled 'manicure,' by the way."

Maggie looked at the piece of paper. "Hey, I can't take credit for this. I wish I could, but it wasn't me. Okay, who did this?" She looked around at everyone.

"Whatever," said Devon, obviously not believing her. "I'll kill you if you ruined my eyeliner."

Maggie dropped the note on the floor like it was a hot potato. "It wasn't me! I'd be the first to admit it if I had thought of something so brilliant. But I didn't do this. I swear. Ask Chris. We were stuck in Senior Lodge."

"That's true. Maggie's been with me ever since rest hour. Boo was there too. Whoever did this must have been in the cabin during the rainstorm," I reasoned.

"One time at school, this girl I know dressed up like a—," Laurel-Ann started, until Boo put her hand over Laurel-Ann's mouth to shut her up.

Betsy picked up the note. "Hey, I know. Let's do a handwriting analysis. Maggie, copy these exact words over on another sheet of paper. Then we can analyze both notes."

We all looked over her shoulder at the handwriting. It was written in capital letters on a piece of Pine Haven stationery. Just about anyone could have done it.

"Fine. Be happy to," said Maggie. "I know I'm the prime suspect, and I'll submit to handwriting samples, fingerprinting, DNA—whatever you want. But I didn't do it. I'm completely innocent."

"Well, okay," said Betsy. "But if you didn't do it, who did?"

"I don't know. Who's the first person who found it?" asked Maggie.

"We were," said Shelby. "Kayla, Laurel-Ann, and I came in right after the rain stopped, and we found it. Then Devon walked in after us."

Maggie pulled on her gorilla socks and climbed up to her top bunk. "Then you're the guilty ones. Case closed."

"We didn't do it!" Shelby protested. "We don't have anything against Devon."

"Well, I don't either," said Maggie, and when everyone laughed at that, she went on, "I don't hate Palechild. I just can't stand her."

When none of us could stop laughing, Maggie said, "There's a difference! There is!" She grinned at Devon, and Devon just fluttered her eyelashes. She was sitting on her bottom bunk, sorting through her makeup bag.

"I don't even care. It's not like you hurt my feelings. Why don't you just admit to it?" She took out her eyeliner and lip gloss and held them up to inspect them.

"Because I didn't do it!" bellowed Maggie. "For the umpteenth time! I *wish* I'd thought of it. Maybe I should just say, 'Okay, I did it,' so you'll all get off my case."

"But Maggie, if you didn't do it, who did?" asked Betsy.

"You tell me."

We all looked around at one another, and I noticed a lot of eyes were falling on me.

"I was with Maggie and Boo," I said defensively. "Anyway, why would I do it? Devon and I are friends." The minute I said that, I felt bad. It made it sound like I thought Maggie was the obvious culprit because she and Devon *weren't* friends.

I turned to Devon. "I didn't do it. Honestly. I know how you feel about your lip gloss."

Everyone laughed, but I hadn't meant it as a joke. I glanced around at the others. "Anyone ready to admit to this brilliant joke?" I asked.

But everyone kept quiet, and we were all looking at each other, waiting for someone to step forward.

I was seriously expecting someone to say something. Obviously, Maggie was the logical suspect, but I knew she couldn't have done it.

I looked at Maggie sitting on her top bunk. She was combing the fur on her gorilla socks, a habit she had because she knew it drove Devon crazy. It looked like she was grooming a couple of black terriers stuck on the ends of her legs.

"Maybe Devon did it to herself," said Maggie, from her perch above the rest of us. "Any of you Sherlocks think of that?"

Devon looked up at us. "Yeah, right. I would never waste makeup like that."

We all cracked up over that comment. Even Devon couldn't keep from smiling this time, although she tried very hard not to.

Still, I couldn't help wondering. I knew Maggie hadn't done it.

So who had?

CHAPTER 10

Saturday, June 21

"Devon, for the last time, don't come near me with that thing," I warned.

"Chris, you might like it. Just let me do one strand."

Devon waved her hair straightener around in front of me, but I backed away. "No. Absolutely not," I said firmly, so she gave up and went back to straightening her own hair instead.

We were in Middler Lodge, along with about five or six other people who were getting ready for the Camp Crockett dance. Since the cabins didn't have electrical outlets, the lodge was the one place we could plug in hair dryers and straighteners.

Shelby and Kayla were with us too, and while Shelby waited a turn to borrow Claudia Ogilvie's hair dryer,

Kayla sat at the piano pushed up against the far wall and played a classical song that sounded familiar. Her fingers rippled up and down the keyboard, never missing a note.

"Wow, you're good," I told her. I liked Kayla, but she was sort of reserved.

"Thanks. It's horribly out of tune, though."

"Hey, Devon, could I borrow your hair straightener when you're done? I've never tried it before," said Brittany, a girl from Cabin One.

"Of course. Your hair will look amazing when you're finished," Devon told her. Brittany already had fairly straight hair to begin with, so I didn't really see the point, but who was I to discourage experimenting with a new look today?

Everyone was so excited about the dance, even though the counselors were acting like they didn't know why so many girls were standing in lines for the showers. It was a little mind game they played about whether we were actually having a dance tonight.

I was glad to borrow Claudia's hair dryer, because it took forever for my thick hair to dry. Ordinarily, I didn't mind just running a comb through it a couple of times and letting it air dry, but today I was paying a little more attention to my appearance.

In just a few short hours, I'd be seeing Maggie's brother, Jackson.

"If I can't touch your hair, can I at least do your makeup?" asked Devon.

"Okay," I agreed, "but keep it light. I don't want to overdo it."

"Don't worry. I happen to be an expert at this," said Devon.

"I know. I trust you," I told her. I sat still on one of the wooden benches and closed my eyes. Devon's makeup brush stroked my face, and I tried to keep from scratching my nose. Kayla's playing was nice background music while we got ready.

It had been really fun spending the afternoon with Devon. Even though she had complained for fifteen minutes about the lack of hot water in the showers, she was obviously as excited as I was about the dance coming up.

Maggie was getting ready too, but she just wasn't as into the whole preparation as much as Devon and I were. We'd left her back in the cabin to get dressed.

"Is your lip gloss okay after that little incident yesterday?" I asked, as I sat there with my eyes closed. Devon was brushing eye shadow on my eyelids.

"Yeah, it's fine. Gorilla Face didn't screw up any of

my makeup. In fact, I couldn't tell that anyone had used it at all."

"Devon, honestly, I don't think Maggie did it."

Maggie was pretty smart, despite the cutting remarks Devon was always making about her intelligence, but that prank didn't seem like the kind of thing she would've thought up on her own. She'd probably want me in on something like that.

"So these Camp Crockett guys—are some of them actually cute?" Devon asked.

"Definitely," I said. "Some of them are totally gorgeous."

With my eyes closed, I tried to picture Jackson's face in my mind. It had been a whole year since I'd seen him, but I could still remember the way his soft blond hair fell across his eyes. He had blue eyes like Maggie, but the resemblance pretty much ended there. His hair was as straight as hers was curly.

This year he was a JC, a Junior Counselor. That's what Camp Crockett called their version of CATs. Like Pine Haven's CATs, JCs weren't in charge of any campers yet, but they had more status than just regular campers.

"Listen, you and I should hang out with Maggie tonight," I said.

"Open your eyes, and do your lips like this," Devon

instructed, opening her mouth so that her lips were parted. "And I refuse to be seen in her presence tonight. It wouldn't surprise me in the least if she wore her favorite hairy socks to this dance."

I parted my lips while Devon stroked on the lip gloss. When she was finished, I said, "You remember me telling you that Maggie has an older brother who goes to Camp Crockett? His name is Jackson, and he's sixteen."

Saying Jackson's name out loud made my heart squeeze. I knew he was too old for me. *Now*. But in a few more years, the age difference wouldn't matter at all. Like when I'm eighteen, he'll be twenty-two. That's not so bad.

Devon made a gagging noise. "A male version of Beefaroni? That's really disturbing."

"He doesn't look that much like her," I assured her. I told Devon about how the Camp Crockett JCs and the Pine Haven CATs always supervised at the dances, so we could spend the whole night talking to Jackson—as long as we stuck close to Maggie.

I could actually feel my heart beating faster while I talked about Jackson. I didn't know him that well, but I could tell he was a fantastic guy. Maggie said he'd been elected president of his junior class for the coming year, so he was obviously a real leader. And popular.

There was something else I had wanted to tell Devon all day, but so far I hadn't gotten up the nerve. I took a deep breath. "I have a huge secret to tell you, okay?" I said softly.

The sound of Kayla's playing made it hard for anyone else to hear me. Devon paused, waiting for me to go on.

"I kind of have a major crush on Jackson." I could feel my face getting warm.

Devon held her makeup brush in one hand and stared at me. "Oh, yeah?" she said, in a tone of complete disbelief. I knew she was picturing an obnoxious, loud redhead covered in freckles.

"Yes, and don't sound so skeptical. Just wait till you see him. And don't you dare say anything to Maggie. You know I can't trust her to keep this secret."

"Don't worry," said Devon. Brittany was finished using her hair straightener, so she unplugged it. "Of course you can't trust your ape friend, but your secret's safe with me."

"Great," I said, letting out a relieved sigh. "I'm glad I told you."

Back at the cabin, Maggie was dressed and ready to go.

"What do you think? Do I look presentable for the

big event?" For the first time all week, she wasn't wearing Jackson's old Camp Crockett hat. She had on a cute pair of jeans and a white polo with thin stripes of blue, purple, red, and green.

"Great outfit," I assured her. I knew Maggie didn't like dressing up at all, but I thought it was fun.

Tonight I was wearing a new skirt I'd just bought with some of my birthday money. It was pouffy and had four different shades of color, from dark red at the bottom, to a hot pink, followed by a soft baby pink shade, and at the top an even paler pink. With it I wore a pink cami with a lacy trim. I loved the fact that I'd never worn this outfit before, and that Jackson would be the first one to see me in it.

Devon for once didn't go for her usual black-and-white look. She had on a dark red V-neck shirt and white capris. With her black hair and fair skin, the red looked amazing.

"That's a great color on you," I told her. "You should wear red more often."

"Thanks." A slight smile played across her lips. It had taken a whole week, but at last there was going to be an event that Devon would enjoy for a change.

"Oh, shoot!" wailed Betsy, dropping to her knees and cupping something on the floor in her hand. "I just

lost a button. I really wanted to wear this shirt tonight."
She looked up at us from the floor. "Does anyone have a
needle and thread?"

Maggie held up her finger and looked thoughtful.
"Actually, I might. My mom packs the weirdest stuff in
my trunk in case of, quote, 'emergencies.' Let me check."

She rummaged through her trunk. "Eyedropper.
Why would anyone ever need an eyedropper? Band-
Aids. A pair of tweezers. Four toothbrushes, three nail
files—half of this stuff I've never even seen before. Oh
wait—what's this?" She held up a little box and shook
it. "Personal sewing kit!" She handed it to Betsy with a
smile.

"Oh, great, thanks!" said Betsy.

"Thank my mom. Just leave it anywhere on my shelf
when you're done."

Then Maggie went to the mirror to brush her hair,
and I went over to stand beside her, acting like I was
checking out my hair too.

"Nice skirt, Kachina. You look like one of those
whatchamacallit dancers," said Maggie.

"What—you mean flamenco dancers? I guess it does
kind of have a Latin flair to it." My skirt wasn't as long
and full as a flamenco dancer's, but I knew she meant it
as a compliment.

"Think we'll see Jackson tonight?" I asked, trying to keep my voice steady. I felt like everyone could hear how much I liked him just by the way I said his name. Jackson, Jackson, Jackson.

"Probably. He wrote me yesterday and said the JCs would be there tonight."

My heart thumped happily. "Uh, I was thinking that Devon could hang around with you and me tonight," I said softly. "I mean, it's a dance, so it's not like there can be some big disaster—nobody falling out of a canoe or anything."

Maggie laid her brush down on the shelf and sighed. "I guess. Chris, I don't mind if you spend time with *her* tonight. I can just talk to Jackson and some of his friends. I'll be okay on my own."

"Maggie, no!" I shouted, and Devon and Betsy both looked at me. "I'm not going to desert you tonight. Let's just try and see if the three of us can't get through one night together. I bet we can. Going to a dance is not like going to activities."

Maggie glanced over her shoulder at Devon, who was sitting on her bed, putting some earrings on. "What if Ghosty Girl refuses to get within five feet of me?"

"Don't worry about that. I already talked to her, and

she agreed that it would be okay for the three of us to stick together. Like Musketeers."

"More like Stooges," Maggie said. Then she made a face like Curly and started dancing around me. "Nyuk, nyuk, nyuk!" From her bed, Devon looked over at the two of us and frowned.

"Enough with Curly already. Can you stand being in Devon's presence tonight?" I asked. The thought of having to referee those two had me a little worried. I was hoping to give Jackson my undivided attention.

Maggie stopped dancing around me. "Sure. I promise I'll be good. I know how it stresses you out when we're at each other all the time."

"Okay, good. I just want to have fun tonight. That's all I care about."

As I stood in front of the mirror, I let out a relieved sigh. I wasn't going to have to split myself in half tonight by spending time with the two of them separately. We were going to be together, all three of us. *And* I was going to see Jackson.

Everything was set up for a perfect evening.

CHAPTER 11

Or not.

Jackson had gotten even cuter since I'd seen him last summer. He was taller, and his face had cleared up. A girl would have to be blind not to fall for him. And Devon happened to have 20/20 vision.

After dinner, we'd all piled into the vans and trucks to go over to Camp Crockett. I'd been in such a great mood. I sat between Devon and Maggie on the bench of one of the vans, and even though they didn't talk to each other, I was able to talk to both of them, and nobody was arguing.

Then we walked into Camp Crockett's dining hall, where all the boys were waiting. All the chairs and tables had been pushed back and stacked up against the walls to leave room in the center for dancing. The boys were all standing around, trying to look cool, and the girls were falling all over themselves to get a good look at the selection that Camp Crockett had to offer.

"Finally," Devon said. "I can't believe I've gone a whole week without seeing any boys."

When I saw Jackson standing across the room talking with a group of Crockett JCs, he actually took my breath away. He was wearing torn jeans and a navy blue shirt with a white seagull on it. That dark color looked perfect on him.

"Oh, there's my brother," said Maggie, in a totally normal voice. Apparently, she had no idea how cute he was. I just hoped nobody would slip on the puddle of drool I was leaving on the floor in front of me.

I loved the way he stood with his arms crossed, the way he laughed, the way his blond hair fell across one eye.

"Let's go say hi," said Maggie. She was so casual. I was feeling a little light-headed, maybe because my pulse was beating faster than a hummingbird's wings.

"Okay," I said, my voice cracking a little. We started moving through the crowd of people around us. Boys were slowly coming over to talk to some of the girls,

♥ 103 ♥

but all these guys were our age. I looked right through them. There was only one boy I could see in the entire dining hall.

"So where's your crush?" Devon whispered to me. I was afraid Maggie might hear her, but Maggie didn't seem to notice.

"See the guy with blond hair in the navy blue shirt?" I asked, pointing as discreetly as I could. "That's Jackson."

"*That's* the gorilla's brother?" Devon gasped, and the second I heard her voice, I knew there was trouble. "Oh. My. God. Not much of a family resemblance, is there?"

Jackson smiled when he saw us approaching, but already I had this panicked feeling, like someone had sucked all the oxygen out of the room. Maybe it was because Devon suddenly bolted a few steps in front of me as we got closer.

"Jackers!" Maggie yelled, and tackled him with a hug.

"Hey, what's up?" Jackson said in his deep, smooth voice. He reached out and wrapped one arm around Maggie's shoulders.

"Remember my friend Chris? I think you guys met last year. And this is Devon."

That's all it took. *This is Devon.*

It was like someone had shot off a starting pistol, because Devon was out of the gate and galloping full speed ahead to capture Jackson's complete, undivided attention.

"Wow, cool shirt! It's Hollister, right? I *love* Hollister."

Jackson smiled. This cute, lopsided smile out of one side of his mouth. A smile that was directed at Devon, not me. "Oh, yeah? You've got good taste. You like to shop there?"

"Yeah, I do. I love how *soft* their T-shirts feel. Hey, you could be a model for them. You've got that California look," said Devon.

Jackson smiled again. Meanwhile I had become completely invisible. I was as see-through as the Converse high-tops I'd had on earlier.

"So are you a counselor? What's your activity?" Devon asked, tossing her head a little so that her hair bounced around.

"He's just a JC," Maggie said. "He's not a counselor. Yet." She reached up and playfully messed up his hair.

"Yeah, I'm not a counselor, but all the JCs assist at an activity. So I help out with swimming." Jackson leaned against one of the tables that had been shoved out of the way of the dancers.

His friends had all wandered off when we had showed up, but Jackson didn't seem at all bored talking to us. He was so friendly and so nice. But my tongue was plastered against the roof of my mouth, and I couldn't think of a single thing to say. Meanwhile, Devon couldn't keep her mouth shut.

"Oh, cool. Are you a lifeguard? Have you ever had to save anyone who was drowning? Give them CPR? Mouth-to-mouth?"

Jackson laughed. "No, luckily! Because I'm lifeguarding at a boys' camp, remember?"

"Hey, you're welcome to come lifeguard at Pine Haven anytime," Devon said with a smile. She looked at me like she was waiting for me to say something, but I just glared at her.

How could she do this? How could she think of so many things to say to him? How could she be so funny and confident? And how could she steal all his attention?

What was she thinking? She knew I liked him, and here she was yakking nonstop and not letting me get a single word in!

That was how the night started, and it didn't get any better. In fact, it got a lot worse.

It seemed like everyone in the dining hall faded into

the background, including me, and there were only two people standing there in a little pool of light, chatting away. Devon and Jackson.

Maggie had promised me she'd be nice to Devon tonight, and unfortunately, she was keeping that promise. I was dying for her to say something that would embarrass Devon.

When Devon was oohing and aahing over Jackson being on the swimming staff, why couldn't Maggie have chimed in, "Yeah, Ghosty Girl here won't go near our lake because she thinks it's a swamp. But Chris is a great swimmer. Like yesterday, she was wearing this cute striped bikini and . . ." But Maggie was on her best behavior. For once.

Devon blabbed her stupid head off. I stood there listening to it all, amazed that she didn't need a few puffs from an oxygen tank every now and then, considering the workout her lungs were getting. Every time she made some funny comment, she'd look at me, like she expected me to laugh at it. I couldn't believe it!

They talked about everything. Jackson being class president next year. "That sounds *great*! Oh, and the junior class officers get to plan prom for the seniors? That sounds *amazing*. Have you picked a theme? Blah, blah, blah, blah, blah, blah, blah."

Picked a theme? How did Devon know to ask all these questions? I figured she'd heard her older sister, Ariana, talk about all this prom garbage. Even if I'd had a chance to get a word in edgewise, I'd never know what kinds of *prom* questions to ask.

The worst part of it was that I had to stand there with a smile on my face, listening to her drone on and on.

Then the subject turned to driver's ed. "Did you do behind-the-wheel training? Yeah, my sister's going to do that too. Oh, can I see your license? Wow, great picture! Do you have a car?"

When I thought things couldn't get much worse, Devon started showing off her "Look at me, I'm in the gifted program" vocabulary. She somehow managed to use the word "audacity" in the course of their conversation.

"Hey, I could use your help studying for the SATs," Jackson told her.

It wasn't like Jackson was really into her or anything. He was just being nice. But it enraged me the way Devon completely dominated all of his attention when she knew I liked him.

I gave Maggie a nudge with my elbow. Couldn't she call Devon "Palechild" right about now?

"Having a good time?" she asked me over the sound of the music.

"No! I wish Devon would shut up!" I whispered hoarsely in Maggie's ear. I didn't want Jackson to over-hear me.

"You think you're gonna throw up?" Maggie practically screamed.

Devon and Jackson stopped talking and looked at me. "That's not what I said!" I shouted. "I did NOT say I was going to throw up!"

"I sure hope not. That would ruin everyone's eve-ning," said Devon, laughing this silly little laugh. After she caught her breath, she was off and running again about what Jackson's favorite music was.

"Really? You play guitar? I should've guessed. You look like the rocker type. Ever thought of starting your own band?"

I wished for a pair of cymbals right about now. Crash them right in front of her face and leave her too stunned and deaf to say anything else for the rest of the night.

I hated every single second of that dance, and it felt like it lasted for thirty-seven-and-a-half years.

When we said good-bye to Jackson, all I could do was fake a tiny smile and get a "See you later" out in a croaky voice. For a second my throat tightened, and

I had to turn away quickly because I was afraid I was actually about to tear up.

I felt like a twenty-pound weight was sitting on my chest. Twenty pounds of sheer disappointment. What did it matter that I'd worn my new skirt? I could've worn striped clown pants and Jackson would never have even looked in my direction.

"Wow, what a great dance," Devon said, when the torturous night was finally over. It was dark outside now, and the night air felt chilly after we'd been crammed inside the dining hall for an eternity with all those loud-mouthed people. All the Pine Haven girls were slowly filing out onto the dining hall porch and down the steps to the parking area.

"Your brother's cool," Devon told Maggie in this annoyingly cheerful voice that made me want to push her down the stone steps. Then finally she noticed that I was still alive. "Did you have a good time, Chris?"

I stopped walking and spun around so that Devon practically crashed into me. "No. I did not have a good time. How could I when my so-called best friend had the *audacity* to talk his ears off for the entire night! I'm surprised you didn't sprain your stupid tongue!"

CHAPTER 12

"What's wrong? Are you mad?" asked Devon. Her stupid mouth was slightly open, and she had this ridiculous surprised look on her face.

All around us, girls were saying good-bye to the guys they'd danced with, and everyone was getting into the vans and trucks to go back to Pine Haven. I was shivering a little because my bare shoulders were cold. But my face felt red-hot from the fury that had been building up inside me all night.

"How could you spend all night talking to him?" I yelled. "You completely dominated the whole conversation! You think he wanted to sit there and listen to you flap your gums all night?"

I heard Maggie beside me, snickering at my comment,

but all my attention was focused on Devon, who was still staring stupidly at me.

"What are you talking about? I was *helping* you. I kept the conversation going! I was waiting for you to jump in anytime, but you just stood there like a zombie whose tongue had turned to dust. If you like a guy, Chris, you have to say more than hello to him."

"You like *Jackson*?" asked Maggie, like Devon had just suggested I liked cold cream-of-mushroom soup. "Since when do you have a crush on my brother?"

I spun around and glared at Devon. "Oh, my secret's safe with you, huh? Thanks a lot! Why don't you go find Jackson and make your announcement to him, too?"

"Why didn't you ever tell me you had a thing for my brother?" Maggie asked.

I closed my eyes and gritted my teeth. "Maggie, stay out of this if you know what's good for you. Let me talk to Devon."

Maggie knew all the warning signs of my volcanic temper. "Okeydokey. I'll see you in the van." She disappeared, and now I was able to give Devon my undivided attention.

"I was doing you a favor by talking to him, Chris. If I hadn't been there, you two would've walked up, said hello, and then left. I happen to be a good conversationalist, so I kept us near him all evening. It's not my fault you didn't say anything all night."

"How could I, with you blabbing your head off! You practically threw yourself at him! Why didn't you just sit on his lap? When Maggie hugged him good-bye, you looked like you were waiting in line!"

We stood in the shadows under the lights outside Camp Crockett's dining hall. Moths were fluttering around just over our heads, and Devon held her hand up to swat away one that was dive-bombing her. Considering how much she'd opened her mouth all night, it was amazing she hadn't swallowed the poor insect.

Devon had this annoying smile on her face. "I did not throw myself at him. You're just jealous because he was talking to me all night instead of you."

"He's not into you, Devon!" I yelled. "He's sixteen and you're only twelve. You think he's in love with you now or something because you used *audacity* in a sentence!"

Devon smirked at me. It was an actual smirk, and I wanted so badly to rub her face in the wet grass and wipe that smirk right off. "Well, he's not into *you*, either. At least I talked to the guy. I can't help it if I made more of an impression on him than you did."

"You're a horrible friend! I can't believe you did that to me tonight."

Devon crossed her arms. "Stop yelling," she said, in a perfectly calm and rational voice that made me want to scream my lungs out. "You're making a fool of yourself."

That comment actually took my breath away. "I—I'm making a fool of myself? Do you have any idea how stupid you looked?" I made a prissy face and put my hands on my hips. "Audacity!" I chirped in a high-pitched voice. "Look how smart I am, Jackson."

Then I thought of something. A way to really embarrass Devon and get her to wipe that smirk off her face. A smile spread slowly across my face. "Devon, why didn't you speak Spanish to him? Why didn't you say *helado* and *sobacos*, huh? You think you're so cool, swearing in Spanish. Well, guess what?"

Devon sucked in her breath. She could tell I was up to something, and she was waiting to hear what. "All you've been saying is a bunch of random words. 'Ice cream' and 'armpits.' That's all. Why? *¡Porque tu no hablas español, gringa! Yo soy bilingüe y tu no eres.* Go ahead—tell me what I just said. You can't, can you?"

Devon was absolutely silent, staring at me. Finally, in a small voice, she said, "That's mean."

Out of the shadows, Betsy came running up to us. "There you are! Hey, come on. The whole van's waiting for you two. Wayward sent me to look for you."

Devon pivoted on one foot and took off at a fast pace right behind Betsy. I followed a few steps behind them. Inside the pit of my stomach, I felt this white-hot coal still burning inside me. All the lava had spewed out and erupted, but deep inside I was still smoldering. My face felt sweaty with the cool breeze blowing on it.

The sliding doors of the van were open, and everyone's faces were lit up from the ceiling lights overhead. Maggie was on a bench by herself with two empty spots waiting.

Devon scooted in front of Betsy and climbed into the van first, taking a seat on the bench next to Kayla and Shelby. That meant Betsy and I would have to sit next to Maggie on the middle bench, which was absolutely fine by me.

I slammed the sliding door shut and slid back onto the bench. My arms gripped my stomach. Neither Devon nor I had said a word.

"Where were you?" asked Gloria. "Kissing your new boyfriends good night?"

"Yes, that's exactly what we were doing," said Devon, as the van drove away.

CHAPTER 13

Monday, June 23

"Isn't this great?" asked Maggie, looking over her shoulder at me from the bow of the canoe.

"Yeah, it sure is." I tried to force some enthusiasm into my voice. We were on our river trip, and Maggie had been having a blast ever since we'd launched the canoes into the water. I was pretending to have a good time, but I wasn't succeeding.

In fact, I felt sick.

I was still mad about a lot of things, and it was all raging around inside of me like a runaway virus. Part of me just wanted to stay in the cabin and lie in bed with all the blankets pulled up over my head.

But I couldn't do that. I'd risk seeing Devon if I did.

So here I was with Maggie on the river, trying to enjoy myself.

This morning the six of us who were going on the river trip had loaded up in the white truck, with a trailer hitched to the back that held the canoes. It was me, Maggie, Meredith Orr, Patty Nguyen, Abby Harper, and Boo, along with Michelle, and Steve, the river guide. He was a tall, skinny guy with long hair and a scruffy goatee—not exactly crush material, but he seemed to know a lot about canoeing and kayaking.

As our canoes drifted along in single file, I tried to get into the spirit of the adventure. The sunlight sparkled on the surface of the river, and the sound of the paddles dipping in and out of the water was nice and calming.

I watched the way the current rippled over the smooth brown rocks in the shallows along the shoreline. Birds were singing in the trees that lined the banks. But no matter how great my surroundings were, I was still in a rotten mood.

"Hey, Chris—look!" Maggie pointed with her paddle at a water snake darting past us. Its thin green body wriggled in S curves just below the surface, but it kept its head above water as it swam.

"Yeah, that's cool."

Maggie twisted around and looked at me from the bow. "Come on, Chris, cheer up already."

"What do you mean, cheer up? I'm having a great time," I told her.

"Hey, this is your best friend you're talking to. I can tell when something's bothering you. Is it because of Ghosty Girl?"

I dipped my paddle in and out of the water for several strokes before I answered. "Sort of. I don't really want to talk about it."

Some people could get mad and get over it pretty fast. But not me. When I got mad, it was like catching a cold—it wasn't something I was going to get over right away. I was going to be tired of it and want it to be over *days* before it actually went away.

I couldn't help the way I felt. In the past, people have told me, "Don't be mad anymore. Just get over it."

To me, that was like telling someone with a cold, "Just don't cough anymore."

"Maybe I can cheer you up," Maggie said. She turned completely around so that she was facing me and started strumming her paddle like a guitar. "Home, home on the river . . . where the fish and the snakes like to . . . slither . . . ."

"Maggie, watch it!" I yelled. We were coming up to some rippling shallows, and we needed to paddle out to deeper water.

She swung around fast and did a quick draw to pull the bow starboard.

"Stop goofing off," I warned her. I adjusted the life vest I was wearing a little bit so it wouldn't rub against my neck.

"Okay, just don't get mad at me. You don't want to be mad at me and Palechild at the same time."

I didn't answer. I had gotten a little mad at Maggie after the dance when she kept bringing up my crush on Jackson. I finally had to admit to her that I did think he was cute, but she'd better never tell him that or embarrass me in front of him.

Luckily, Maggie was very sympathetic about my fight with Devon. Every time I thought about the way she had taken over at the dance and left me standing there, speechless, while she did all the talking, I felt that hot, burning feeling in my stomach again. It really did feel like I'd been walking around for the past two days with an old piece of smoldering charcoal in my stomach. Most of the time, it was all white around the edges, but when I'd think about Devon saying, *I love how soft their T-shirts feel* or *Oh, can I see your license?* that lump of charcoal in the pit of my stomach would flare up red-hot again.

"This river's pretty tame, don't you think?" Maggie commented. "When are we going to see some real rapids? It's not that different from being on the lake."

"Just pay attention, okay? I don't think we're ready for real rapids," I told her.

I breathed in the river smell all around us. It was a little fishy, but I still liked it. This really was fun. If only I could get Devon completely out of my mind.

Maybe it wasn't all her fault. Maybe she really had been trying to help me out by talking to Jackson.

But she should've noticed she was totally dominating the conversation and leaving me standing there, saying nothing. She could be a real flirt sometimes. I never should've confided in her in the first place. What was I thinking—telling my *best friend* a secret like that?

"So you like being in the stern okay? We could switch places on the next trip, and you could paddle bow, if you want," Maggie said.

"It doesn't matter. Stern's fine with me for now."

And how come Devon had to be so completely comfortable talking to Jackson? I mean, really! She took one look at him and immediately had an entire phone book full of things to say to him.

If I'd planned it for a week, I never could've come up with that many things to talk about. Driver's ed classes, prom, Hollister shirts, guitars. Had she taken a class on how to talk to sixteen-year-old boys and not mentioned it to me?

I could still see her standing in front of me. *I happen to be a good conversationalist.* GRRRRRR!!!

I dug my paddle down as deep as I could and thrust it through the water with all my might.

"I'm glad you and I never fight, Windsoroni," I said suddenly. She gave me a quick grin and then turned back to paddle past a fallen tree branch sticking up out of the water.

The lump of charcoal was feeling hotter and hotter. I wasn't just mad at Devon. There was something else.

Okay, yeah . . . Devon had made me mad, really mad. But she hadn't tried to hurt me on purpose. She didn't even know she was making me mad.

But . . . but then there was the stuff I'd said. I called her a horrible friend. *Yo soy bilingüe y tu no eres.* I'm bilingual and you're not.

"We're coming up to a bend!" yelled Michelle from the lead canoe. "Remember to stay to the inside."

"I think we need to move a little more to the port side," I told Maggie.

❤ 121 ❤

I'd gone out of my way to hurt Devon. I'd made a point of saying something I knew would humiliate her. Telling her that she was only saying "armpits" and "ice cream." My ears felt hot when I thought about it. She must've felt so stupid. And if there was one thing Devon hated, it was to feel dumb over something.

I *knew* that. I'd picked the one thing I could think of at that moment to make her feel bad about herself.

We'd made it around the bend in the river, and a stretch of calm water was ahead of us. We passed a field with tall green grass where some cows were feeding. One black cow looked up, turning her head to follow us as we drifted past. She chewed thoughtfully the whole time she kept her eyes on us.

Maggie mooed at her and slapped her paddle playfully against the water.

"Hey, Maggie . . . do you think I'm a mean person?"

Her head turned sideways a little, and I could see she was smiling like she couldn't believe I'd ask such a crazy question. "Of course not. You don't have a mean bone in your body."

Oh, yeah? How did she know that? The third metatarsal on my left foot was mean. And my tibia could be downright cruel sometimes.

Yo soy bilingüe y tu no eres. I'm bilingual and you're not.

I'd never done that before. Said something mean in Spanish to someone who spoke only English. Just to make her feel stupid because she wouldn't know what I was saying.

"Well, what if I did something mean to you. Would you forgive me for it?"

"Sure, I guess so. If you apologized and I knew you didn't really mean it."

Apologize.

Apologies had a way of getting stuck in my throat. They wouldn't come out. I couldn't say them. Something about apologizing made me feel like all my skin was being peeled off. I just couldn't stand to look someone in the eye and say, "I'm sorry. I did something wrong."

Maybe I could write a note. Try to make it funny, but still basically say I was sorry.

But then she'd better be ready to apologize to me, too. I never would've said those mean things if she hadn't been such an *habladora*—chatterbox.

Because she was the one who started it all. So she should be the first to apologize. Maybe I would say I was sorry if she'd say it first.

"Do you think Devon and I should try to make up?" I asked Maggie.

"Well, in some ways, it's kind of nice to have Ghosty Girl out of the way," Maggie admitted. "Can you imagine having her along right now? You'd be back in the stern and she'd be up here with her nose stuck in a magazine. You'd crash right into a rock!"

I laughed. It felt good to actually laugh about something again. "There is no way Devon would ever have come on a river trip!"

Maggie had a good point. I hadn't planned it that way, but fighting with Devon did give me an excuse to spend all my time with Maggie now.

At least I still had one best friend.

CHAPTER 14

Tuesday, June 24

"Oh good, you're just in time," Laurel-Ann said when Maggie and I walked into the cabin. "The laundry's here, and I want everyone to help me sort it, but Boo said to just get my own stuff out and leave everyone else's alone. I think I should—"

"Stick a sock in it!" Boo yelled at Laurel-Ann, throwing a pair of my striped socks at her head. The two of them were on Side A, and the big canvas laundry bag with everyone's clean clothes was sitting on the floor by Wayward's bed.

Devon was there too, lying on her bed, reading. She hadn't even looked up when Maggie and I walked in.

I'd tried writing her a funny letter yesterday. I was going to apologize for everything I'd said after the dance. But I lay there on my top bunk, staring at the blank piece of paper. I ended up scribbling out everything I started to say. It was hard to concentrate, knowing she was lying on the bunk below me.

I didn't feel so mad at Devon anymore. Now I was worried. The longer we went without speaking to each other, the worse things got. I just needed to apologize. But what if she wouldn't accept my apology?

"Nobody wants you touching their underwear, Hyphen," Boo was saying. "Just let everyone find their own stuff." Boo scooped armfuls of clothes out of the bag and dumped them on Wayward's bed.

On Sunday afternoons, every cabin would stuff all their dirty laundry into these big bags, and then a few days later, the clean clothes would come back. It was a lot easier for ten people to throw all the dirty stuff together than it was to sort the clean stuff out into ten separate piles.

Maggie and I went over and began rummaging through the pile of clean clothes, along with Boo and Laurel-Ann. Meanwhile, Devon hadn't moved. Maybe if I found some of her clothes, I could take them to her. Would she thank me? Ignore me? We'd barely made eye contact for the past three days.

There had to be some way I could start talking to

her again. The note idea was a great one, but I couldn't write anything half as good as Devon had written me. If I couldn't think of the right words to put down on paper, how could I ever come up with the right words to say?

I grabbed my pink shorts and purple sweatshirt from under the bottom of the pile. I saw a pair of black jeans, but I wasn't sure if they were Devon's or not.

"There's my Camp Crockett jersey," said Maggie. She pulled it out of the stack and let out an earsplitting shriek.

Laurel-Ann screamed too. "It's alive!" Something black and fuzzy was stuck to Maggie's jersey. "It's alive, it's alive!" Laurel-Ann took two big bounces and landed on top of Maggie's nearby trunk. She wouldn't stop screaming.

"My gorilla socks!" Maggie held the red jersey up over her head. Dangling from the armpits were her furry black gorilla socks.

"Hyphen, shut up!" Boo yelled. "It's not alive. It's a pair of socks."

Laurel-Ann collapsed on the trunk. "I thought there was a rat in the laundry bag! It was furry and black and horrible!" She sat on the trunk, making little whimpering noises and tugging nervously on her braids.

Maggie gave one sock a tug. It didn't budge. She held it up for a closer look. "Hey! They're *sewn* on! Somebody sewed my gorilla socks into the armpits!"

The next thing we knew, Maggie fell to the floor and curled up in a ball. She was laughing so hard she couldn't even breathe. Her face turned beet red and her whole body was shaking.

Boo was laughing too. She grabbed Maggie by the shoulder and shook her. "Breathe in! You need oxygen!"

Maggie took one long, shuddering gasp. She beat on the wood floor with both fists. "That is the FUNNIEST thing I've ever seen in my life!"

Even Devon had sat up by now and was looking at all this over the top of her book. I smiled in her direction, but she looked right through me.

Just then Betsy pushed the screen door open and came in. She glanced around and sighed. "Okay, what'd I miss this time?"

Maggie sat up, panting. "Oh! Oh! My stomach hurts! I think I ruptured my liver or something."

I took the red jersey out of her clenched fists and held it up for Betsy to see.

"Interesting," was Betsy's only comment.

On her hands and knees, Maggie crawled across the cabin floor to the edge of Devon's bed. "That was brilliant. Even better than your stuffed body. Up high!" She held her hand up for Devon to high-five her, but Devon wouldn't even look at her.

"What? You think I did it? Why would I bother?" was all she said.

Maggie sat cross-legged on the floor by Devon's bed. "To get me back. Even though I wasn't the one who got you in the first place. I guess we're even now. Although since I never got you, maybe *I* need to get *you* back now." She clutched her head in her hands. "This is so confusing!"

Devon sighed and tossed her book on the shelf. "Let's make something clear. If I'd played this little immature prank on Beefaroni here, I'd be the first to take credit for it. I can't sew, don't even know how to thread a needle, thank you, and I wouldn't waste my time."

I tried smiling at her again, but she still acted like I was completely invisible.

"Hold on, hold on!" Laurel-Ann piped up suddenly. "Maggie's shirt was in the laundry bag, and the laundry has been gone for the past two days, so that can only mean one thing. Nobody in our cabin could've done it; it must have been one of the laundry ladies. But why?"

Boo spun around and looked at her. "One of the laundry ladies came across Maggie's red jersey and Maggie's black furry socks, and said, 'Hey, I know. I'm going to sew these into the armpits'? That's it! Laurel-Ann has solved the mystery!" Boo applauded and whistled.

"Laurel-Ann, whoever did it got to the clean laundry before any of us," I told her. "They took the shirt and socks out and sewed them together, then put them back into the bag. Someone in *our* cabin, not the laundry ladies."

It could easily have been Devon. She'd probably been here alone in the cabin all afternoon. Maybe she did believe Maggie had stuffed her "body" that day, and she'd been waiting for the right time to get her back.

Devon was like that. She was the type to be patient and sit back until just the right opportunity came along. Maybe she'd started looking for her own clothes in the laundry bag, came across those socks she hated so much, and hatched her brilliant plan.

But then she was also the squeamish type. She probably wouldn't want to lay a finger on Maggie's furry socks, even if they had just come back clean from the laundry.

"They're sewn in with just a few stitches of black thread," Betsy said, examining the shirt up close. "Anybody got some scissors? One snip, and they'll be loose."

"No!" Maggie jumped up. "I'm gonna wear it this

way from now on." She took the shirt away from Betsy and slipped it over her head. Then she flapped her arms up and down. "I love it!"

Maggie spun around in circles, jumped up on Wayward's bed, and bounced from the top of one trunk to another. "I can fly!" She raised one arm up over her head and peeked at the fuzzy sock dangling from her armpit. "Anybody got a razor?"

"Anybody got a needle and thread?" I asked. "Who was sewing on a button the other day?"

"Maggie has a sewing kit," said Betsy. "Remember? You let me borrow it when I lost my button."

"That means Maggie did it!" said Laurel-Ann. "But why did she do it to herself?"

"I didn't do it! You guys give me way too much credit," said Maggie. She was climbing up to her top bunk. "You think I'm the one who thought up Ghosty Girl's prank. You think I'm the one who thought up this hairy armpit prank. I'm not that clever."

She leaned out from her bunk and grabbed onto one of the rafters over her head. "I'm part gorilla, remember?" She swung off her bed and hung from the rafter with both hands, making chimp noises while the rest of us cracked up at the sight.

Gloria walked in the door at that moment and

gasped. "Get down from there! You want to break a leg?" It was the most authoritative I'd ever heard her be.

Maggie dropped to the floor and stood up. "I'm okay."

Gloria held a hand to her chest. She looked truly panic-stricken for a minute. "Sorry, I didn't mean to yell at you, Maggie."

Maggie crossed both hands behind her head so the socks were in full view. "Hey, no problem."

None of us could stop laughing at Maggie. Boo told Gloria everything she'd missed.

"Maggie's the only one with a sewing kit," said Laurel-Ann, plucking at the rubber bands on her braces thoughtfully. "But Devon's her mortal enemy. Did Maggie do it to make us think Devon did it, or did Devon do it to make us think Maggie did it?"

Maggie went over to her shelf and picked up the little sewing kit. "Yeah, but it's right here in plain sight. Anyone could've borrowed it. And I don't know how to thread a needle either." She gave Devon a toothy grin while scratching herself under one arm.

"Believe whatever you want," Devon said, picking up her book and hiding behind it again. "It doesn't matter to me."

"I don't think Devon did it," I said. I could feel her looking at me.

"Did you do it, then?" asked Maggie, turning to me.

"No! Why would I do it?" I glanced at Devon, but she'd already turned away.

I wanted her to look up and thank me for defending her. I wanted to sit on the end of her bed and ask her about the book she was reading now, *The Member of the Wedding*.

Last week, before we'd fought, she told me it was great and she'd let me borrow it when she was finished. Maggie had asked her if she was planning her wedding, and Devon had told her she had no concept of great literature.

Everybody was still laughing about the gorilla socks. Who cared about the gorilla socks? I'd lost one of my best friends, and I didn't know how to get her back.

It was one thing to avoid Devon now and hang out with Maggie during camp, but camp wouldn't last forever. How could I get through seventh grade next year without her?

I needed Devon. But from the looks of things, she didn't need me.

CHAPTER 15

Friday, June 27

"See that rock up ahead? We're going to work on eddy turns now, and this can be a little tricky, so listen up." We'd pulled the canoes up on a muddy bank where the river was shallow. Steve had been giving us instructions on how to "read" the river. That meant being able to look at a river's current and see where possible dangers were.

"Okay, notice on the port side of that rock, you can see how the current goes around it?" Steve pointed. "That water is moving downstream, but behind the rock, the current actually swirls around and flows upstream. You see what I'm talking about?"

"The crosscurrents are coming together like this." Michelle held her hands apart and then moved her palms together. "That's the eddy line. You want to pass that rock on the port side and point the bow of your canoe into the eddy line. Then the current will swing your canoe around and you'll be behind the rock, sitting in that little calm pool on the other side of it."

"This sounds complicated," said Patty, tightening the strap of her life vest.

"I'm going to go first. Watch what I do, and it'll make a lot more sense," said Steve. "Who wants to paddle with me?"

"I guess I will," said Meredith. They pushed their canoe off the bank and stepped in, paddling into the current of the river.

Once Meredith and Steve had passed the rock, they spun their canoe around behind it, with the bow pointing back upstream.

"They made it look easy," said Boo, rubbing her glasses on the edge of her T-shirt before putting them back on. I was a little nervous about this maneuver, and everyone else seemed to be too.

"Yeah, they did," Michelle admitted. "If you don't do it right, you'll end up tattooed on that rock instead of going around it."

That comment made us all laugh.

"I kid you not, you guys. Be careful you don't broach

on that rock! If the current does start to suck you too close to it, remember to lean *toward* the rock."

"That doesn't make sense. Shouldn't you lean away from it if you hit it?" I asked.

"No! Lean toward it." Michelle leaned to one side and we all leaned sideways too, laughing and holding our arms out to balance. "Your first impulse is going to be to lean away, but then you'll wrap the canoe on the rock."

Michelle said she'd go last with Patty, so now it was Boo and Abby's turn. Steve yelled directions as they got close to the rock. They had a little more trouble than Steve and Meredith had, but they eventually made it.

"Ready?" Maggie asked me.

"Sure," I said, not feeling at all ready. We pushed off from the bank and started downstream. As we approached the rock, I felt like the current was taking over and pulling us where it wanted us to go.

"Forward sweep, Chris!" Steve yelled at me. "Maggie, do a high brace!"

The water was rushing past the rock, but I leaned forward in the canoe and swept my paddle across the water like Steve said. The next thing I knew, the canoe spun and we slid in right beside Steve and Meredith.

"Awesome! That was beautiful!" Steve put his fingers in his mouth and whistled.

All the tension I'd felt disappeared, and I smiled at Meredith, who gave us a thumbs-up. Maggie turned around and winked at me from the bow.

Michelle and Patty were next, and they did pretty well, but they banged against the rock on their starboard side as they were passing it.

"I hereby present the golden paddle award to Chris and Maggie!" Steve yelled. "I hope you all watched the way they did it, because that was exactly what you want to do."

"Woo-hoo!" Maggie cheered, holding her paddle up over her head. I couldn't wipe the smile off my face. This was the happiest I'd been all week.

Then Steve and Michelle gave us instructions for peeling out of the eddy, and one by one, we took our turn and pointed the bows of our canoes into the eddy line so that we'd swing back around downstream. Pretty soon we were all heading down the river again in single file.

After we'd gone about a mile or so farther, we pulled the canoes over to the bank. We found a shady spot under some trees and ate the picnic lunches we'd brought. Steve and Michelle told us stories about the whitewater rapids they'd run on other rivers. I was loving every minute of this trip.

When we launched the canoes back into the river, Steve told us we were coming up to a place where we'd practice another eddy turn.

"This one's a little trickier than the first one, but everyone did well the first time, so listen up to my instructions when we get close."

"Just watch the experts," Maggie told everyone.

When we got to the spot Steve had been talking about, he and Meredith went first again. It made me nervous to see how close they'd come to this rock. I figured we should keep a little more port side than they had.

Maggie and I were next. "Think we should do it with our eyes closed this time?" she asked, turning around and covering her eyes with one hand.

"No!" I yelled. "Pay attention!" The current was getting faster as we approached the rock.

Maggie let out a fake scream. "We're going to wind up tattooed on that rock!"

"Cut it out!" I yelled again. "Stop playing around and paddle!"

"We're too close to the rock! We're going to crash!" Maggie called, still goofing off. She was doing a draw, which was pulling us closer to the rock.

"What are you doing? Pry!" I yelled. We were getting

too close! I was doing my best to swing us away from the rock, but Maggie was working against me.

We hit the rock with a jarring thud. "Lean into the rock! Into it!" I heard Steve yelling.

The current swept us sideways, slamming us broadside against the rock. Automatically, I leaned away from the rock which made the canoe tilt sideways. A spray of water hit my face. Water was pouring in over the gunwales. We were filling up fast.

"Get up on the rock!" Steve bellowed at us. I scrambled out of the canoe and clutched that rock like my life depended on it. Maggie was right beside me.

Steve was on the opposite side of the rock, shouting directions to us. "Forget the canoe! Save yourselves!" He was pointing to a spot near the rock where he wanted us to jump in and then get to the shore as fast as we could. We were only about ten feet from the riverbank, and the water was calmer there.

I slid off the rock into the freezing water. The current felt like it was going to sweep me downstream, but my life vest kept my head from going under. I did a couple of hard strokes until I was in shallow water. I grabbed hold of some tree roots sticking out of the riverbank and pulled myself up on dry land. Mud oozed between my fingers, but I didn't care. I'd made it out of the water.

Maggie lay panting on the bank next to me. Before I knew it, everybody else was all around us. I wasn't sure how they'd all maneuvered that eddy turn and gotten over to us so fast.

My legs wouldn't stop shaking. I lay there on the muddy bank, flat on my stomach, pressing my whole body into the wet ground. I didn't dare try to sit up; my heart was pounding too hard.

Maggie turned over on her back. She was gasping for breath. Her hand swept up over her forehead. She looked at me lying beside her. In a weak voice that sounded like a drowned kitten mewing, she said, "I lost my hat."

"You lost *your hat*? Who gives a flip about your hat? You lost your brain!" I screamed at her.

Now I was sitting up. "Your brain is sailing down that river right now, Maggie! It's bouncing off every rock out there! Fish are eating it for dinner! You stupid show-off! If you hadn't been goofing off out there, that wouldn't have happened!"

Maggie sat forward with her head in her hands. "I know, Chris. It's all my fault. I'm sorry, okay? Don't be mad at me."

I leaned over and rapped on her skull with my knuckles. "Knock, knock! Who's there? Nobody! Time

❤ 140 ❤

to put up a vacancy sign!" I was yelling so loud it hurt my throat.

Maggie raised her arms up over her head to shield herself. "I'm sorry," she wailed. She looked up at me, and tears were streaming down her cheeks.

"Chris, you're bleeding," I heard Patty say beside me.

Then I noticed my knees. Both of them were scraped up, and a bloodstain was spreading slowly across the right one, making a criss-cross pattern of bright red in the skin. The left one wasn't bleeding so much.

"Oh wow, I didn't even see your knees," Patty said, leaning over me. "I was talking about that cut there."

She pointed to where a long, scarlet ribbon of blood was oozing all the way down the side of my leg into my clear Converse sneaker.

"I'll get the first aid kit," said Michelle.

Once she got the kit from her canoe, she dabbed my bloody leg and knees with some clean gauze. I hadn't even felt my cuts and scrapes when I was in the cold water, but now they were stinging like crazy. I was shivering too because I was dripping wet, and even though I tried to hold still and control it, my teeth wouldn't stop chattering.

I could hear Maggie sniffling nearby, but I refused to look at her. I felt like bursting into tears myself from all the trauma I'd just been through. But I kept my eyes focused on Michelle's hands patting my knee dry, and that kept the tears from starting up.

"This one looks pretty nasty, but it's not deep, just long. You won't need stitches, at least," she said about the long gash on the side of my leg. It ran from just below my knee almost to my ankle—a bloody cut about six inches long.

Everyone was standing over me in a circle, still wearing their life vests, holding their paddles and watching Michelle work on me.

"How'd it happen?" Meredith asked.

I shrugged, not trusting my voice. I still wasn't sure I could keep from crying. I had that achy feeling at the back of my throat.

"Probably when you climbed on the rock," said Michelle. "It was pretty jagged and rough." She put Band-Aids on my knees, but there wasn't one long enough for the cut on my leg.

"Does it hurt?" asked Abby sympathetically, bending down beside me.

"Not much," I managed to say. "The water numbed it at first."

"Maggie, you okay over there? Got any scrapes that need patching up?" asked Michelle, looking over at

Maggie sitting by herself, her paddle across her knees.

She shook her head and didn't say anything. Her hair was still wet from our plunge into the river.

Steve came walking up the bank, and his wet shirt was clinging to his chest. He'd been on the rock, looking at how to get our canoe off it where the current still had it wrapped.

"You ladies sit tight. This is going to take us awhile," he told everyone.

While he and Michelle got ropes and worked on getting our canoe unpinned, everyone else stood around me. Nobody had said anything to Maggie, but everyone seemed concerned about me.

"Want a water bottle, Chris?" asked Boo, holding one out to me.

"No, I'm okay."

"Want me to rinse the blood out of your shoe?" Abby asked. I looked down and noticed the blood drying on the inside of the clear plastic.

"Thanks, but that's okay."

It seemed like hours until Michelle and Steve came back up the bank, wet and exhausted, but they'd managed to get our canoe off the rock.

"Will you be okay paddling the rest of the way to the pickup point?" Michelle asked me.

"Yeah. Can I paddle with you?" I asked, my voice cracking a little.

"Of course." She patted my back. I picked up my paddle and walked past Maggie without looking at her. She could paddle with Steve or walk back to camp for all I cared.

Luckily, we didn't have much farther to go to where Roy, Pine Haven's chubby maintenance guy, was waiting for us with the white pickup and the trailer.

"I'll get that for you, Chris," said Meredith, when I tried to help Michelle lift our canoe up on the rack.

We climbed into the back of the pickup, which had a bench running along the sides and the back. I sat between Boo and Meredith, as far away from Maggie as possible.

"I always feel like a horse when I ride in the back of this truck," Patty commented. The truck bed had a top over it and wooden slats on the sides, and once we were on the road, the wind whipped our hair around our faces, and everyone had to shout to be heard over the noise.

But I wasn't talking. Neither was Maggie.

CHAPTER 16

"You'd better go to the infirmary and let the nurse clean those cuts up a little more," Michelle told me as soon as we got back to camp. They didn't even expect me to stay and help put away all the life vests and paddles or unload the canoes from the trailer.

I went to the cabin to change out of my wet clothes before going to the infirmary. Since it was the middle of the afternoon and everyone was still at activities, the cabin was empty. Except for one person.

Devon.

She was lying on her bottom bunk reading, all by herself. When I realized we were going to have to face each other, I almost felt like turning around and walking out again, but she'd already seen me.

She just glanced at me and went back to reading without saying anything. I dug through my duffel for some clean, dry clothes.

"Oh my God! What happened to you?" Devon said suddenly. She was sitting up, staring at the bandages on my knees.

"I got this beauty too," I said, turning sideways so she could see the dark red gash on my leg.

She gasped and came over to take a closer look. "That looks terrible! What happened?"

"Maggie and I broached our canoe on a rock. I got cut up while we were scrambling around on it. We had to climb out and swim to shore."

"Wow! That sounds awful!" Devon stood with her arms folded over her stomach, like the sight of my wounds made her woozy.

"It was all Maggie's fault! She was playing around, pretending that we were about to hit the rock, and then we did!" I pulled a clean shirt over my head and ran my fingers through my damp, tangled hair.

"Did she get hurt?" asked Devon.

"No. Of course not! There's not a scratch on her." The next thing I knew, I was spilling the whole story to Devon, telling her about what a great job we'd done on the first eddy turn, but then Maggie had to go and be a show-off and get us wrapped on a rock.

"Oh my God! That sounds so unbelievably dangerous! You're lucky it wasn't worse. She could've gotten both of you drowned!"

"I know, right?" I felt so much better now that I was telling Devon about what happened. I didn't mention how I'd yelled at Maggie and pounded her skull with my bare knuckles. She kind of had it coming to her. Maybe.

"You'd better disinfect those cuts immediately. Who knows what kinds of bacteria you picked up from that river?"

"Oh yeah, I'm supposed to go to the infirmary to get these cleaned up."

We looked at each other. "Are you still mad at me?" I asked in a soft voice.

Devon looked down at her dingy white sneakers. "I thought you were mad at me."

"Well, I was. For a while. But I'm not anymore. You haven't been talking to me, so I didn't know if I should talk to you."

Devon wouldn't look at me. "Same here."

"Well, I hated it when we weren't talking. It's been a whole week!"

"I know. I've been counting every day," said Devon, flicking her eyes up at me in a quick glance.

"So have I!" I said. A warm feeling of relief spread over me, like I'd just been wrapped up in a soft blanket.

"Look, I'm sorry I talked to Jackson so much. I can see why you got mad at me. I knew you liked him, and I should've backed off. You looked great that night, by the way."

"Really? Thanks!"

"Yeah, you really did. Your hair was beautiful—don't ever straighten it. And your makeup was perfect, if I do say so myself. Plus, I loved that skirt you were wearing."

Now it was my turn. I should just say it. Tell her I was sorry for all those mean things I'd said. Apologize for embarrassing her and telling her the wrong Spanish words. And flaunting the fact that she wasn't really bilingual.

But Boo and Maggie walked in the door right at that moment before I could get the words out of my mouth.

"Hey, I want to talk to you," Devon said to Maggie. Boo winked and made a scared face at me. Then she went straight over to her side of the cabin without a single comment.

"Do you know you could've killed Chris? Have you

lost your mind?" She stood with her hands on her hips, glaring at Maggie.

I almost laughed at that; Devon and I really did think alike. Would she tell Maggie her brain was floating down the river?

Maggie looked around Devon at me. "I'm sorry, Chris. I'm really sorry you got hurt." Her voice cracked when she said it, and her bottom lip quivered.

All of a sudden, I felt like I was on the verge of tears again. If Devon hadn't been there, I might have lost it. The whole thing had been so scary. I wanted to yell at Maggie some more. But then I wanted to tell her I hadn't meant to rap on her head with my knuckles and say all those things about her missing brain. It was just a total reaction to the terror I'd gone through.

"Leave her alone! You've done enough to her already! Your sheer stupidity has always annoyed me, but I never realized how dangerous it was." Devon turned to me. "Come on, Chris. I'll take you to the infirmary."

CHAPTER 17

Monday, June 30

"It has to be one of the Side B girls. They're getting us one by one. First you, then Maggie, and now Betsy. I suppose I'm next," I told Devon.

We were sitting cross-legged on her bottom bunk, playing chess. Everyone else was at afternoon activities. Warm sunlight was pouring in through the window screens, and I could hear June bugs outside, buzzing in the trees. But here we were, inside.

"Whatever." Devon shrugged. "I just don't get this fascination with childish pranks." She moved her bishop and took my pawn.

"But don't you think they're funny? I saw you smiling over Maggie's gorilla socks sewn to her jersey." I moved my rook to the seventh rank, attacking multiple pawns and preventing the king from coming out.

Devon pressed her lips together firmly to keep from smiling. She pretended to be concentrating on her next move, but I could see that dimple in the corner of her mouth. She moved her rook so she could take control of the open lines.

Last night as we were getting ready for bed before lights-out, Betsy's retainer case was missing. She always kept it on the shelf by her bed. When we found it on a shelf above Wayward's bed, she opened it to find red, smiling lips inside.

"I've been pranked!" Betsy had shouted. "Somebody actually cared enough to play a prank on me! Thanks, whoever you are!" Then she'd taken the big red lips out of the case and held them in front of her mouth. They were made out of the same clay stuff we'd used in crafts to make our plates. Also inside the case was a tiny, stamp-size note in teensy writing that said, *A kiss from the tooth fairy.*

And still nobody was taking credit for it. Betsy seemed excited to be included in the pranks, but she was worried about where her retainers really were, until she felt something under her pillow and discovered a little box made out of popsicle sticks.

The retainers were inside it, along with another

tiny note: *B: Keep those pearly whites straight! TF*

"Boo seems like the most obvious suspect, don't you think?" I asked Devon, moving my queen to take her pawn but still keeping my eye on the back rank mate.

She was completely focused on our game. She took it very seriously, and she almost always beat me. She moved her pawn, attacking my knight. But I couldn't move it because it was pinned to the rook.

"Yeah, I guess. Pay attention to your knight."

I moved out of the pin, and she took my knight. "I mean, Boo has that sarcastic sense of humor. Laurel-Ann, well, she's just not the type to play pranks. It could be Shelby. Or even Kayla. Kayla's pretty quiet, but you get the sense that she's watching everything and making a note of it."

I could tell Devon wasn't that interested in this conversation. But like everybody else in the cabin, I was curious about who was behind the pranks. The Side B girls denied everything. They were convinced that Maggie and Devon had pranked each other. But none of them had a good explanation for why Betsy was the latest target. It definitely put a new twist on things.

I leaned forward. "Hey, tell me the truth," I said softly, not that anyone was around to hear. "Are you responsible for the gorilla socks prank? You can tell me. I'll keep your secret."

Devon didn't look up from the board. She rested her chin on one hand, trying to figure out her next move. I waited impatiently for her to answer me.

She moved her bishop into position against my king and sat back, a satisfied look on her face. "There. Check."

I moved my king out of check. "Well, did you?"

"Did I what?" she asked, moving her knight in, planning to fork the king and queen but also threatening a forced checkmate in two moves. There was no way I could stop it without losing my queen. She hadn't even heard my question. Or was she pretending not to because she was the guilty party?

"Did you sew Maggie's gorilla socks onto her jersey?"

Devon rolled her eyes. "As I've said before, do you think I know how to thread a needle?" Then she crinkled her nose and added, "Do you honestly think I would ever lay a finger on those hairy things Beefaroni puts on her feet?"

She had a point there.

"I think it's Boo. I wonder what she's going to do to me."

Devon shook her head. "Who cares? Will you make your move, please?"

I moved my rook to prevent mate.

Hanging out with Devon for the past few days had given me a taste of how she'd been spending all her time while I'd been busy going to activities with Maggie. We'd spent the morning in the cabin reading. Devon was thrilled that she now had someone to play chess with, but I couldn't get over feeling like I was missing something.

Friday afternoon I'd switched from not speaking to Devon to not speaking to Maggie almost instantly. It was like I could only be friends with them in shifts. I probably would've talked to Maggie by now, but Devon was always by my side, and I felt like she was shielding me from getting close enough to Maggie to speak to her.

Maggie had taken the hint and was off doing things on her own. I was glad I'd made up with Devon, but I hated spending all my time in the cabin when there were so many other things to be doing.

Where was Maggie right now? She was definitely outside on this beautiful summer afternoon.

Devon moved her knight, forking the king and queen. "Check." She tried not to smile, but she was obviously pleased with her performance.

I moved my king out of check. After her knight took my queen, my rook took her knight. We exchanged rooks. Then Devon brought her king into the center, rounding up the pawns.

I moved my king into the center too. She had already rounded up the pawns and had a pawn past the fifth rank. I couldn't stop it, so it promoted to a queen.

She then boxed my king in on the last file. I had to move my king because it was the only piece I had left. She then moved her queen to g2 and said "Checkmate," smiling.

"Good job," I told her.

"Want to play again?" she asked.

"No, you already beat me twice." I moved all the chess pieces off the board and flipped it over. It folded in half and served as a carrying case for the pieces. "What should we do now?"

Devon fell back on her bed, her head on her pillow. "Want to read for a while? How far are you in *Brave New World*?" Devon had let me borrow that book to read, but I wasn't too into it yet. It was a good book and everything, about a futuristic world where everyone was controlled by the class they were born into, but I wanted to be *outside*, doing things.

"Not that far, really. I don't want to read anymore.

My eyeballs need a break. Let's go to an activity now, okay? How about archery? You liked that the last time."

Devon sighed. "It's too hot. There are too many gnats. It's too far to walk."

Maggie would never let gnats keep her from having fun. I stood up and went over to the window to look out. The sunlight was making a pattern of light green and dark green on the leaves outside.

I turned around to face her. "Devon, come on. Let's do something." It was one thing for us to hang out in our rooms back home and do nothing on a summer afternoon, but precious camp minutes were ticking away.

Last night at assembly in the lodge, Michelle had announced that another river trip was coming up on Thursday. Maggie and I had kind of looked at each other, but we hadn't said anything. Now that my knees and cut had scabbed over, I wasn't so mad anymore.

I needed a chance to talk to her alone. Without Devon around. But Devon was always around now. There had to be a way I could make up with Maggie but still keep Devon as a friend. Wasn't it possible for me to be friends with both of them at the same time?

My birthday wish hadn't come true. No matter

how hard I tried, I couldn't be friends with Maggie when Devon was around or friends with Devon when Maggie was around. I felt like I was caught in a tug-of-war.

I wondered how long it would take until I was pulled in two.

CHAPTER 18

Wednesday, July 2

When the rising bell rang, I couldn't force my eyelids open. I felt shivery, so I pulled the covers up around my neck. Five more minutes. I just needed five more minutes of sleep.

"Wake up, sleepyheads!" I heard Gloria call from the other side of the cabin. She was always the perkiest in the mornings.

"Don't worry, I'm up! On school days, I wake up at five forty-five because I have to catch my bus by seven o'clock, so I'm used to getting up early. In the winter, it's still dark outside when I wake up. It's not hard to wake up once it's light outside, don't you agree?" Laurel-Ann was chattering away like a squirrel, and I wished I could throw my pillow across the cabin to shut her up.

"Whoa! *Righteous!*"

That made me open up one eyelid to see what was going on.

Wayward was sitting up in bed, holding a black top hat. "This is the sickest piece of headwear I've ever seen in my life!"

Maggie sat up and swung her legs over the side of her bed. "Where'd *that* come from?"

Wayward put the top hat on her head like it was a crown and then climbed out of bed and went to the mirror. She stood there in her pink boxers and tank top, gazing at herself.

Betsy sat up and squinted at Wayward in front of the mirror. "What's going on?"

Wayward turned around and looked wide-eyed at all of us. "Abe Lincoln's ghost. He must have visited me in the night and left me this hat." She turned back to the mirror. "I love Abe Lincoln's ghost. He is one stylin' dude."

By now, the Side B girls had figured out something was up with us.

"What's going on over here?" asked Boo. She came over in her flannel pajama bottoms and T-shirt and stared at the hat on Wayward's head. Laurel-Ann, Kayla, and Shelby had crowded in behind her.

"Hey, where's your regular hat?" asked Maggie, climbing down from her top bunk and scooting across the dusty wooden floor to Wayward's bed. The nail over Wayward's bed was empty. She always hung her plaid hat on it before she went to sleep.

Wayward looked around at Maggie and shrugged. "Don't know. Don't care. *This* is my hat now."

"The phantom prankster has struck again!" Maggie announced. She plopped down on Wayward's bed and bounced up and down on it.

Boo glanced at Laurel-Ann. "Those laundry ladies keep picking on our cabin."

"It's not the laundry ladies! I get it now. You don't have to keep reminding me," Laurel-Ann insisted. Her long hair hung down around her shoulders, unbraided.

"I have one question. Where on earth did this phantom prankster find a black top hat?" Kayla asked.

"I know! The dress-up trunk in Junior Lodge. There's all kinds of weird clothes and costumes in there," said Boo.

"Hey, come on, everyone. You still have your chores to do before inspection," Gloria reminded us.

"Okay, but we have to find out who's responsible for this!" Laurel-Ann's voice was so shrill it made my head ache. "First Devon, then Maggie, then Betsy, and now Wayward. That means the logical suspect is . . . Chris!"

I groaned and covered my head with my pillow. Why was everyone talking so loud? My back ached, and no matter how I shifted around, I couldn't get comfortable.

"Chris? Come on, time to get up." I heard Gloria's muffled voice beside me and felt her patting my back.

I removed the pillow and looked at her. "I don't feel so great."

"What's wrong?" she asked me. "Are you sick?" She put her hand on my forehead, and her palm felt so cool and soft.

"You're warm! I think you have a fever."

Now I was suddenly the center of attention as everyone crowded around my bed.

"I think you need to go to the infirmary," Gloria said softly. "Can you get up and get a few of your things together? I'll walk you down there."

"I'll go with her. I've been there before," Devon announced, throwing a dirty look in Maggie's direction.

Maggie looked at me with the same sad eyes she'd been watching me with for the past few days. I could tell she felt sorry for me and wanted to say something.

I wanted to tell her I wasn't mad anymore, but

♥ 161 ♥

everyone was standing around, and they were all talking, and my head was throbbing.

Meanwhile, Devon was gathering up my toothbrush, hairbrush, and some clean clothes from my duffel and putting them in her little overnight bag to carry to the infirmary.

"Can't I just stay in bed?" I asked Gloria. "All I want to do is sleep."

"The nurse can give you something for your fever. And you may be contagious, so it's better to move you to the infirmary," Gloria told me.

Wayward stood beside her in that ridiculous top hat. "The nurse rocks. She has popsicles."

Somehow I managed to climb down from the top bunk, but my head felt heavy, like an oversize watermelon swiveling around on my neck. Devon handed me a robe. Everyone was watching me, and the cabin was too crowded and noisy. The sound of Laurel-Ann's breathing made me want to give her a shove, but I restrained myself.

Devon and I walked out of the cabin, and the cool morning air felt sort of comforting, but I couldn't stop shivering. We walked down the hill toward the infirmary beside the camp office. My flip-flops were sliding in the dewy grass.

On the dining hall porch, Eda was ringing the bell for breakfast. The thought of food made me suddenly nauseated. I hoped the nurse wouldn't make me eat anything.

When Devon and I opened the screen door to the nurse's office, she pursed her lips and looked concerned. "You two? Again? What do I need to bandage this time, Miss Ramirez?"

"My head hurts, and my back. And I think I have a fever," I moaned, sinking into the wooden chair next to the scales. Nurse Linda was a nice blond lady who always wore scrubs. She opened a drawer and pulled out a digital thermometer. Devon leaned against the wall and waited.

"Open up," she said, sticking it under my tongue. When it beeped, she pulled it out. "Oh, my—100.8. Let's get you into a bed."

It was the first time I'd been inside the actual infirmary, past the nurse's office. Five single cots were lined up in a row, all with fresh white sheets on them. The wooden walls were painted a pale sickly green. Or maybe I just thought it looked terrible because I felt terrible.

Devon had followed us from the office to the infirmary, but Nurse Linda looked over her shoulder and said, "I'll take it from here. You'd better get to the dining hall."

So Devon handed me the bag with my stuff and left, and I crawled gratefully into one of the beds.

"I just sent Gracie Arbuckle back to her cabin last night after two nights here, so you're my only patient. But this has been going around—fever, chills, headache, body aches. It's viral, so there's not much I can do but give you something for your fever."

She tucked me in and came back in a few minutes with some pills and a paper cup of water. I swallowed them and then sank back into bed and closed my eyes.

I didn't open them again for what felt like days. I slept and slept. The nurse tiptoed around and checked on me every now and then.

Sometime in the early afternoon, she brought me a cup of ginger ale on ice and some saltines. It was the coolest, most delicious drink I'd ever had in my life. And the saltines were amazing too. I licked all the salt crystals off to savor their flavor. Then I plopped back into bed and fell immediately asleep.

The next time I woke up, I was completely disoriented. I'd forgotten where I was, and I thought it was morning for a few seconds. When Nurse Linda saw that

I was awake, she came over and took my temperature again: 99.3.

"Better, but that doesn't mean your fever won't go up again when the acetaminophen wears off. How about a Popsicle?"

The buzzer sounded, which meant there was somebody in her office, ringing for her to come back.

"Uh-oh, I hope that's not another feverish patient." She left to go answer the buzzer, and I lay in bed, curled up on my side. My back still felt achy.

Nurse Linda opened the door from the office and peeked in at me. "It's a visitor for you. And she brought a friend of yours." She was holding Melvin.

I sat up in bed and smiled. "Is it Devon? Can she come in for a few minutes?"

"No, it's not Devon. And you're contagious, so she can't come in. You can say hi to her through the window screen."

I crawled out of bed and went over to the window screen to peek out. If it wasn't Devon, it must be . . .

"Hi, Maggie," I said. My voice sounded rusty.

"Hey, how ya feeling?" she asked. She had to look up to see me because the height of the window was over her head.

I pressed my forehead against the screen. It smelled

dusty and metallic. "A little better. Thanks for bringing me Melvin."

"Sure. He didn't want to sleep without you tonight." She smiled and stood there for a few seconds. "Are you still mad at me, Chris?"

"No, not anymore." I tried to think of what to say next. It didn't help that I felt all wobbly, and my head was hurting again.

"Well, I just wanted to say I'm really, really, *really* sorry that I made us broach on the rock. It was all my fault! And you got those cuts and scrapes and everything. I'm such an idiot sometimes. My brain really did go floating down the river that day."

Hearing that made me cringe. All the mean things I'd said came rushing back to me. "You're not an idiot, Maggie. Honestly—I'm not mad anymore. I was going to tell you that today, if I got a chance."

I cleared my throat and tried to think of how I wanted to bring up what I'd said. About the vacancy sign in her head and everything.

"Hey, Wayward's still wearing that top hat around. She's had it on all day! And we all think Boo's the guilty one. She swears she isn't, but none of the rest of us knew that the Juniors had a trunk full of dress-up costumes in their lodge—did you?"

"Nope, I don't think I've ever even been inside Junior Lodge."

"I know! Boo's like, 'Hey, I can't help it that I'm the only one who's been coming to Pine Haven since I was eight.' So mystery's solved, don't you think?"

"Sounds like it. I'm glad nobody's blaming me just because I'm the only one who hasn't been pranked. So far." The screen made Maggie's face blurry.

"Oh, yeah! I almost forgot to mention—I'm even being nice to Devon today!"

"Really?" I laughed. "That's hard to imagine."

"Well, we both miss you. Think you'll be out of there tomorrow?" Maggie asked, gazing up at me.

"I'm not sure. I hope so. I guess it depends on if this fever goes away."

"Well, I hope you'll be back tomorrow. If I'm nice to Devon, you can hang out with both of us at the same time. That is—if you want to hang out with me again."

"Of course I do!" I told her. I cleared my throat again. I should say something.

"Okay, well . . . see you later!" Maggie waved and stepped away from the screen.

"Hey, Maggie?" I called, pressing my nose against the screen. "Uh . . . I just wanted to say . . . thanks. For coming to see me. And bringing me Melvin."

She grinned. "No problem." Then she turned and jogged away before I could say anything else.

I went back to my bed and crawled between the sheets, hugging Melvin tight. His little red flannel nightcap covered up one eye, and his red bear tongue stuck out at me. The sheets felt so cool and delicious, and I pulled them close around my chin.

Okay, so I'd wimped out of telling Maggie I was sorry. But then, she didn't seem to be expecting me to apologize. I could write her a note when I got back to the cabin. That way I'd be able to think of exactly the right words.

I chuckled at the thought of Devon and Maggie actually getting along for a change. I'd have to see that to believe it.

Friday, July 4

Late in the afternoon, the nurse decided I was finally well enough to leave the infirmary. I hadn't had a fever all day. I walked back to the cabin by myself, wondering what everyone was up to.

Since it was the Fourth, the whole schedule today had been different. I'd already missed a lot of fun stuff, but at least I was getting out in time to see the fireworks over the lake tonight.

I could hear voices coming from the window screens as I got close to Cabin Four. One of them sounded like Maggie. And then I heard Devon laugh. I sped up a little and pushed the screen door open.

The cabin was dark after the bright sunlight outside,

and my eyes had to adjust for a second. All I could see were silhouettes.

"Hey! Look who's here!"

"How are you feeling?"

I blinked and looked around. Betsy was sitting on her bottom bunk, smiling at me, and I was sort of aware of Laurel-Ann and Kayla on Side B talking to Gloria.

Then the strangest sight in the world met my eyes.

Maggie.

And Devon.

Sitting together on Devon's bottom bunk.

"Glad you're back. You won't miss the fireworks," Devon said cheerfully, leaning back on one arm.

Maggie sat cross-legged next to her. "Yeah, you should've been here for the counselor hunt. Nobody caught Wayward. That's three straight years she's gone without being caught, and she's worth fourteen points!"

"But we did catch Tisdale in Cabin One, and she was worth seven points, so that helped," said Betsy.

So I'd missed the counselor hunt, a kind of camp-wide hide-and-seek where the campers all looked for the counselors, and each cabin could score points based on how many years the counselors they found had been coming to Pine Haven.

"Yeah, and we beat the Seniors this morning in the capture-the-flag game," Maggie said. "The strategy of distraction, right?" She gave Devon a fist bump.

Devon smiled. "Strategy of distraction. It worked, too, didn't it?"

The back of my throat felt raspy and dry. Strategy of distraction? What was that all about?

Something weird was going on. I wanted to walk out of the cabin and check the sign by the door to make sure I'd walked into Cabin Four. Because it was starting to feel like I was in the twilight zone.

Devon and Maggie, sitting together on Devon's bottom bunk. Bumping fists. Laughing and talking. *Together.*

"What's going on here?" I said finally. I'd dropped the overnight bag with my stuff in it at my feet. I was holding Melvin by one furry paw.

Maggie looked up at me with her eyebrows arched. "What do you mean?"

I couldn't think of how to explain how weird this whole scene was. Was this a leftover symptom from my fever? Was my brain just not working completely normally yet?

"You . . ." I glanced over at Betsy on her bunk, and she looked back and shrugged. "What . . ." Maggie and Devon waited for me to finish my sentence.

"Why are you sitting there?" I finally asked, pointing an accusing finger at Maggie.

"What are you talking about?" She swung her legs around so she was facing me. "You sure you're feeling okay?"

I held my hands up and then dropped them at my side in exasperation. Melvin bounced against my thigh. "You two are actually talking to each other?"

"Oh, wow, you really have been gone for a while," Devon commented. "Maggie and I are friends now."

"Friends?" I asked, like Devon was speaking in Lithuanian.

"Yeah, we've been hanging out together. And guess what? I'm a vegetarian now. Devon's teaching me all about it," Maggie added with a big grin.

"Vegetarian?" I asked. Another foreign word I was hearing for the first time. I hoped my jaw wasn't touching the top of my purple and red high-tops.

"That's right," Devon put in. "Veggeroni here hasn't eaten anything with a face for three days."

Had I heard that right? Did Devon say *Veggeroni*?

"Yeah, you know, I've always thought it was cool that you're a vegetarian. You didn't believe me at first when I said I was going to try it out myself," Maggie told Devon.

Devon shrugged. "Sorry I doubted you." She looked up at me. "You remember the day you went to the infirmary? At lunch, Maggie ate the tofu and veggie stir-fry."

"See, Chris! I told you I was being nice to Devon for a change! Plus, we were both lonely without you."

I didn't say anything. Both lonely without me, huh? Well, at least they were able to keep each other company.

"At first I thought she was setting me up for some big joke. I was really skeptical," Devon went on, telling me the fascinating story of how the two of them became friends. "But she kept asking me questions, really good questions about how to keep a balanced diet, and how to deal with temptations . . ."

"Like bacon!" Maggie added.

"And I realized she was truly interested in becoming a vegetarian. Plus, it's like you've been saying—she's a lot smarter than I ever realized."

Maggie fluttered her eyelashes in a Devon imitation. "And she also appreciates my sense of humor now."

Devon couldn't keep from smiling. "She really can crack me up at times. Remember that joke you told last night about—."

"I'm not in the mood to hear a joke right now!" I snapped at Devon.

Maggie looked at me sympathetically. "You still feeling a little sick?"

"Yeah, I'm still feeling a little sick," I said in a loud tone.

Devon leaned forward. "I know what will make you feel better. You should join us. Boycott the hot dogs tonight and eat the pasta salad and baked beans instead."

She and Maggie were both smiling like they'd just joined a zucchini-eating zombie cult.

"I like eating animals that have faces!" I shouted. I threw Melvin onto my top bunk and he bounced before landing on his back.

Devon and Maggie both stared at me, and Betsy snorted and then started coughing to hide her laugh.

"But Chris, just try it for a day. There are so many non-meat foods available, and Grainy Girl has taught me all about . . ."

I had no idea what Devon had taught Maggie because that "Grainy Girl" name came sailing through my left ear and got lodged in the middle of my brain. *Veggeroni? Grainy Girl?* They'd made up new pet names for each other?

"I'm eating a hot dog tonight and that's final!" I heard some crazy person yelling in a voice that sounded like my own. "Leave me alone!"

I turned and shouted at Betsy. "What time do we eat?"

She shrank back a little and glanced around. "Uh, six thirty. We're having supper on the hill tonight, buffet-style." Then she swallowed like she hoped I wouldn't yell about anything else.

"And they're serving hot dogs? Great, I'm starving!" I glared at my two best friends with flames shooting out of my eyes. "I'm definitely having seconds."

CHAPTER  20

Saturday, July 5

There was no doubt about it. I'd stepped out of the infirmary yesterday and into the twilight zone.

I'd only been gone for three days, but in camp time, that was about equal to a month. And during that time, something radical had happened.

The earth must have tilted on its axis. East was now west, up was now down, and Devon and Maggie, my two best friends who couldn't go for more than five seconds without insulting each other, were now friends.

And not just mild acquaintances. They'd bonded like superglue.

In *three* days.

Last night as we'd sat out on the hill eating supper,

I'd had to listen to more "how we became friends" stories from Devon and Maggie.

Maggie had definitely been the one to make the first move. She'd been worried about how the three of us would get along when I came back from the infirmary. Somehow, sharing menu ideas made them connect in a way I never thought was possible.

They both kept telling me how much they appreciated each other's sense of humor now—*suddenly*. I sat there, gobbling down two hot dogs while they ate their baked beans and told their stories.

I started to get the impression that if Maggie and Devon had been left alone from the beginning without me in between, maybe they would've been friends from the start.

And even though I should've been happy that they were finally friends, I couldn't help feeling like I was now in their way. As I'd watched the fireworks last night over the lake, I'd had this disturbing feeling that I was watching my friendships with Devon and Maggie explode.

Now it was Saturday morning, and the three of us were on our way to the tennis courts. That was another thing that had apparently happened while I was gone. Devon and Maggie had been playing tennis together, and suddenly Devon was Venus Williams or something.

"You really need to start reading labels. Lots of things you think sound vegetarian might have animal by-products in them," Devon advised.

"Really? Like, what does that mean, exactly? Animal by-products?" The two of them were walking side by side, swinging their rackets. I was a couple of steps behind them. I was waiting to see if either one of them would notice I was even there.

"Well, for instance, tomato soup. Sounds vegetarian, right? It could be made with chicken broth, and you'd never know it if you didn't check the label for ingredients."

"Are you kidding? Chicken broth in tomato soup? Weird! So have you never eaten meat in your whole life?" asked Maggie.

"Oh sure, my parents fed me meat till I was eight. Then I put my foot down and insisted on a cruelty-free diet. I plan to raise my kids as vegetarians. If they choose to eat meat when they're older, so be it. But at least they'll have a choice I never had."

"I admire that," Maggie commented. "Maybe I should do that with my kids too."

"Devon, maybe you should name your firstborn Asparagus, and Maggie, you can call your kid Brussels

Sprouts, or just Sprout for short," I muttered under my breath.

Neither of them heard me over the sound of their own voices.

The night before I'd had the freakiest dream. I was sick in bed with a fever, only I was in the cabin instead of the infirmary. And I was in Devon's bed with white sheets on it. The nurse had just taken my temperature, which, for some reason, was six thirty. She made a point of emphasizing the thirty part and how high that was.

It was all dark and shadowy in the cabin, and I was tossing and turning in bed. The next thing I knew, Devon and Maggie were hovering over me. They had no eyes, only dark sockets where their eyes were supposed to be.

And Maggie was holding a red bell pepper in her cupped hands, and Devon was waving around a gigantic purple eggplant. They were both chanting, "Join us, Chris! Join us!"

I woke up in my own top bunk with my rainbow sheets, drenched in a cold sweat, shaking with terror. It was absolutely horrible.

"You know who else is a vegetarian? Meredith Orr in Cabin Two," said Maggie. "She's gone on river trips with us, and she told us that at lunch one day."

I'd always thought it was cool that Devon was a vegetarian. Sure, I liked meat, but at some point, I could probably give it up as easily as Maggie had.

But there was something so annoying about the way they walked along, swinging their rackets, Maggie with her curly red hair bending closer to Devon with her straight black hair.

It made me hope we were having bacon double cheeseburgers for lunch today. With a fried egg on top.

"Oh good, there's an empty court," said Maggie, pointing with her racket. "Chris, wait till you see how good Devon has gotten in the past few days." Maggie looked over her shoulder at me, suddenly remembering my existence.

"But you and I have been playing singles. We'll have to find another partner to play doubles," commented Devon. "If we can't, maybe the two of us should play Chris."

Maggie smiled at her. "I don't know, that doesn't sound fair. You and I would probably pound her."

That sounded absolutely delightful to me. My two best friends pounding me.

Tisdale, the tennis counselor, said hello to us and bounced some balls in our direction, which Maggie scooped up and crammed into her pockets.

"I wonder what kind of doubles partners we'd be. I bet we'd make a good team," Maggie said to her new best friend.

"True, because your serve is much better than mine, but I'm pretty good playing close to the net," Devon replied to *her* new best friend.

I bent down to grab a stray ball rolling across the court. I felt like shoving it in my ear to drown out the sound of the two of them complimenting each other.

We walked onto the empty court and stood by the net. Nobody else was around who wasn't already playing, so we were missing a fourth doubles partner.

Maggie bounced a ball up and down and glanced at me. "Uh, Chris? Want to just watch for a few minutes? You can see how much Devon's improved lately."

I stared back at her. "Of course. Sounds peachy."

Neither one of them noticed the sarcasm dripping off my tongue. They both skipped away as happy as two peas in a pod and took their positions on opposite sides of the court. I stood leaning against the fence, wondering why I'd bothered to even come along.

There were so many more interesting things I could be doing right now. Picking all the lint off my socks, for instance, or counting the strings on my racket.

But no, I was privileged enough to stand here and

watch while Devon and Maggie played each other in a game of tennis.

That was how I spent my whole Saturday. Watching Devon and Maggie at crafts. Watching Devon and Maggie at archery. But mostly watching Devon and Maggie talk.

I'd almost forgotten that we were having the second dance with Camp Crockett tonight because I'd been having so much fun being a spectator for an entire day.

Late in the afternoon, everyone was lined up outside the showers again and racing around, getting ready. Devon and Maggie made a point of getting in line early, but I took my sweet time collecting my shampoo and soap, so when I got down there, I was way in the back.

"Chris, come up here." Maggie waved to me where she was standing with Devon in line for the third shower stall. "We saved a spot for you."

"No cuts!" yelled Katherine Sperling at me from her place in line.

"I'm okay back here," I told them.

Maybe a cold shower would wake me up from this nightmare.

By the time I got out, Devon and Maggie were waiting for me in the cabin.

"We're going to the lodge," said Devon, waving her

hair straightener around in one hand. "Are you coming with us?"

"No, thanks," I said, toweling my hair dry. "You said I should never straighten my hair, remember?"

"Yeah, but you can come with us and hang out at least," said Maggie.

"Well, I don't want to hold you up," I told them. "You two go ahead, and maybe I'll be down in a few minutes."

"Okay, see you in a few," said Devon cheerfully, and they left together, talking about which brands of shampoo didn't test their products on animals.

Wayward came in and stretched out on her bed. She'd seemed a little down the past couple of days because her old plaid hat had reappeared and the black top hat had magically vanished.

Betsy ran a brush through her short blond hair. "Looking forward to the dance tonight?" she asked me with a friendly smile.

"Sure. I guess."

Not even the thought of seeing Jackson tonight could perk me up right now. I had no idea what I was going to wear. I could wear the same outfit as last time, since he'd never even laid eyes on me, but instead I just settled on a pair of jeans because my knees still looked all scabby. Then I grabbed the first clean shirt I saw, an orange tank top.

No way was I going down to the lodge to interrupt Devon and Maggie's friend fest. They'd never even miss me.

About twenty minutes later, Devon walked in with a big smile on her face. "Attention, everyone. I'd like to present to you the new and improved . . . Maggie Windsor!" She held the screen door open.

An unrecognizable person with absolutely straight red hair walked in.

"Ta-da!" shouted Devon.

The redhead had an equally big smile on her face. Kayla and Laurel-Ann came running over.

"Oh my gosh! Maggie?" gasped Laurel-Ann.

Devon stood with her arms crossed, a satisfied look on her face. The redhead was standing in front of the mirror, turning from side to side to admire the view.

She looked at all of us. "What do you think? Different, huh? I kinda like it!" She turned back to the mirror and looked sideways at herself. "I can't wait till Jackson sees it! He'll freak!"

Devon nodded. "It's the new you!"

Betsy, Laurel-Ann, and Kayla stood around and complimented this stranger on how she looked. Boo walked in and burst out laughing, but then she admitted she thought it was a nice change.

"It's an awesome new look," Wayward said with a sigh. "Be better with a top hat, though."

The new Maggie stood in the middle of the crowd and grinned. She looked so completely different.

I felt a sudden pang in my heart.

I really missed the old Maggie.

CHAPTER 21

When the dance started in Pine Haven's dining hall a few hours later, my mood hadn't improved. Jackson did look cute and everything. He had on a gray T-shirt and plaid shorts, but he was so stunned by the sight of his sister with straight hair that he never even noticed me.

"And I'm a vegetarian now!" Maggie announced, after he got over the shock of her hairstyle. Then Devon and Maggie told him all about that, and I walked away and pulled up a chair. Might as well get comfortable.

Devon frowned and gave me a quick, one-handed wave that meant *Get back over here*, but I looked away and watched the dancers for a while.

I could hear Jackson telling them a story about how he'd had to help a counselor pull some kid out of the lake today after he'd hit his head on the diving board. "Don't worry, though. I didn't have to give him mouth-to-mouth! He was breathing and everything."

Even Jackson's rescue story wasn't enough to get me to walk over and stand there with them while the three of them talked.

I left three times to get bug juice and cookies, went to the bathroom twice, wandered out to the porch once, and watched Reb Callison and another girl from Cabin One, Kelly Hedges, get into a screaming fight.

It was a thrill-packed evening.

After the Camp Crockett guys had left our dining hall, we were all walking back up the hill toward the cabins. Devon ran through the crowd to catch up with me.

"What's wrong with you? I was going to help you talk to Jackson, but you sat by yourself the whole night."

"I don't feel well," I told her.

Maggie came up on the other side of me so they had me surrounded. "You're not feeling well? Sorry to hear that." She patted me on the shoulder, but I moved away. I didn't want to be comforted right now.

The tree frogs were croaking like crazy, and the smell of the just-cut grass filled my nose. An occasional lightning bug flicked on and off around us. I was glad they couldn't see my face in the dark. My eyes were watering a little, and my nose tingled. I had this heavy, sad feeling in my heart, like everything had changed and nothing was ever going to be the same as it was before.

Maggie had new, straight hair. Devon liked her now, and Maggie liked Devon. And neither one of them seemed to care at all about how I felt about any of this.

All I wanted to do was go to bed. Maybe tomorrow I would start to get used to this new arrangement. All summer I'd felt like each of them had me by an arm, pulling me in opposite directions.

But now, suddenly the two of them were a perfect pair.

And I was the third wheel.

I was the first one in the cabin, and I flipped on the light switch at the door. Yellow light flooded the room, making me squint. I went to my duffel and pulled out the oversize T-shirt I slept in.

"Wasn't he cute?" Laurel-Ann squealed from Side B. "His name is Eric. I love that name now! Think he'll call me when camp is over? I gave him my cell phone number three times and he said he'd memorized it. It's easy to remember because of the 4477 part at the end.

Don't you think that's an easy number to remember?"

"Unfortunately, it's permanently imprinted on my brain," I heard Boo tell her.

I stepped up on the metal rungs at the end of the bunk bed and saw a sheet of paper lying on my pillow.

A note from Devon saying she was glad I was back?

I picked it up and started reading. It was written in all capital letters on Pine Haven stationery.

WE HAVE YOUR BEAR. DO NOT, WE
REPEAT, *DO NOT* CONTACT THE AUTHORITIES.
IF YOU WANT TO SEE YOUR BEAR ALIVE AGAIN,
YOU WILL MEET THE FOLLOWING DEMANDS
BY SUNDAY EVENING AT SIX P.M. THEN YOU'LL
AWAIT FURTHER INSTRUCTIONS ABOUT
WHERE TO FIND YOUR BEAR.

IF OUR DEMANDS ARE NOT MET, WE WILL
RETURN YOUR BEAR TO YOU . . . LITTLE BITS
OF STUFFING AT A TIME. DO NOT TAKE ANY
CHANCES WITH YOUR BEAR'S SAFETY!

PLACE THE FOLLOWING ITEMS IN A
PILLOWCASE AND LEAVE THEM ON THE
BACK PORCH OF MIDDLER LODGE.

RANSOM DEMANDS:

A long list of stuff followed, and my eyes quickly scanned the rest of the page. My heart was pounding like crazy, and I looked around. Melvin wasn't propped up on my pillow where I always left him. But I noticed something sticking out from under my pillow. It was Melvin's little red flannel pajama bottoms.

"What's that?" asked Maggie, coming up behind me to look over my shoulder.

I crumpled up the paper and hurled it across the cabin in the direction of the trash can. It missed.

"Very funny. Now give me back my bear."

Devon stood beside Maggie. They both stared at me with wide eyes. "What's going on?" asked Devon with this totally innocent tone in her voice.

"Give me my bear back. Now!" I roared at Devon. My heart had turned into a caged animal, beating against my rib cage as if was trying to escape.

"I don't have your bear," said Devon. Her eyes darted from my bed to the trash can to Maggie.

I swiveled around and faced Maggie. "Give him back. It's *not* funny!" The blood was roaring in my ears like ocean waves pounding on the shore. "I'm not in the mood for a joke right now, and I want my bear back!"

Kayla and Shelby were peeking across the cabin at

us to see what all the yelling was about. Betsy came in, holding her toothbrush. "What's going on?"

A hush had fallen over the cabin. I stared down Devon and Maggie. "I'm waiting!" I yelled. Yelling was good. Yelling helped. Being mad kept me from bursting into tears.

Maggie went over to the wadded-up piece of paper lying on the floor and unfolded it so she could read it. She looked up. "I guess the prankster kidnapped Melvin," she said in a soft voice.

"I'm sick and tired of these stupid pranks!" I spun around to glare at all the faces looking at me. "You two think you're so funny, but you're not!" I screamed at Maggie and Devon.

"Chris, maybe it wasn't them," Betsy said in a hushed voice.

"Well, don't everybody start blaming me again. I didn't do it!" said Boo.

"I wish Gloria and Wayward were here," Laurel-Ann whispered to Kayla. But they'd stayed in the dining hall with the rest of the counselors to move the tables and chairs back.

The blood still roared in my ears, and my heart hammered away, going two hundred beats a minute, or at least it felt like it. I knew any second I was going to cry, so I had to do something. Had to make this stop.

I climbed up on my top bunk and thrust my feet under the covers. Everybody's eyes were on me, waiting to see what would happen next.

"I'm not going along with this stupid joke," I announced loudly, staring up at the rafters over my head. My face felt as hot as Devon's hair straightener. "The pranks stop now."

I rolled over so that I was facing the wall. Hot tears spilled out onto my pillow, and I took slow, steady breaths so I wouldn't sniffle.

No one said a word. I could hear them all moving around and getting into pajamas. I closed my eyes and let the tears flow.

CHAPTER 22

Sunday, July 6

When I first woke up, for a split second I didn't remember anything, and I felt completely normal and content. Then it all came rushing back to me.

I sat up and glanced around. No sign of Melvin anywhere. I looked all over our side of the cabin, my eyes scanning the shelves, the trunks, and everyone still lying asleep in their beds.

He wasn't anywhere. I fell back into bed and stared up at the rafters above me. My face felt hot as I remembered last night.

It was just a joke. My bear had been kidnapped, and they were threatening to return little bits of stuffing at a time? I felt the corner of my mouth twitch a little.

Bearnapping. It was kind of cute.

I rolled over and buried my burning face in my pillow. How embarrassing! Everyone else had laughed at the pranks that were played on them. Wayward had fallen completely in love with her new hat; Maggie had ruptured a vital organ, laughing over the gorilla socks.

Betsy had been so excited. *Somebody actually cared enough to play a prank on me!* Even Devon, who thought she was above it all, had been a totally good sport about her prank.

And then I'd blown a gasket.

My face felt like it was burning a hole in my pillow.

How could I face everyone after last night? What could I possibly say that would erase that scene from everyone's minds?

I listened to the sound of birds twittering outside in the trees. Betsy coughed, and I felt the bunk beds rock a little when Devon turned over below me.

It was just that the timing had been all wrong. I was already in a bad mood, and the "ransom" note had caught me completely off guard. I'd been suspecting for days that I'd be the next victim, but when it actually happened, it felt like it came out of left field.

Off in the distance, I heard the gong of the rising bell ringing. Across the cabin from me in her top bunk, Maggie propped herself up on one elbow and looked around. Her hair was not exactly straight anymore, but it wasn't all curly, either.

"Hey," she said to me in a rough, sandpaper voice, "did Melvin come back last night?"

I felt a little laugh come out of me like a hiccup. It sounded funny, like he'd run away on his own and he could find his way back again. "Nope. No sign of him," I said in what I hoped was a completely bored tone.

Today my strategy would be to act like I didn't care, that it didn't bother me at all.

Wayward groaned as she stretched. "I love Sunday mornings." The best thing about Sundays was that there was no inspection, so we didn't have to clean the cabin. Also, we got to go to breakfast in our pajamas.

Maggie climbed down from her top bunk and came over to me, her eyes level with the edge of my bunk. "Hey, Chris. Don't worry. We'll help you get Melvin back. Let's just play along with it and leave the ransom demands like the note said."

I rolled over and let out a big yawn. "Whatever." As casual as I was trying to be, my face still felt warm. I wondered if I was blushing.

I climbed down from my top bunk and slid my feet into a pair of flip-flops. I felt like everyone was watching me, waiting to see if steam was going to shoot out my ears. I couldn't undo that little temper tantrum from last night, but at least I could try to act normal now. What if I laughed about it now? Was it too late for that?

"Oh, that's right! You missed it!" I heard Laurel-Ann's voice rising with excitement. "Last night Chris found a ransom note on her pillow. Her bear got kidnapped, and he's going to have all his stuffing pulled out bit by bit if she doesn't meet the ransom demands!"

I didn't look in her direction, just headed for the door so I could leave for breakfast as quickly as possible, but Gloria came up to me, a frown on her face. "What's going on?"

I sighed and rolled my eyes. "It's no big deal. Just more pranks."

Gloria glanced around at everyone. "Okay, who has the bear?"

I forced a laugh out of my throat. "Don't worry about it. I don't even care." Then I slipped past her and walked out the door.

At breakfast Gloria gave everyone a big lecture about respecting each other's belongings, but Wayward kept telling us to "be Zen" and we'd all get along, so nobody knew how to react.

For the rest of the day, anytime anyone brought up the subject of Melvin, I tried to act like it didn't bother me in the least. But nobody else would let it drop. The entire cabin was now completely focused on the "bearnapping."

Sunday schedule was different from the rest of the week; we didn't go to regular activities. We always had a really big lunch, and then in the afternoon, there'd be crazy games with the whole camp: watermelon seed spitting contests, egg relay races, shaving cream fights, and water balloon battles.

I drifted through the afternoon activities, not really a part of Maggie and Devon's little circle, but not really separate from them either.

Late in the afternoon, right before supper, a bunch of us were in the cabin. It was getting close to six o'clock, the time for me to drop off the ransom demands, but I hadn't said a word about Melvin's disappearance since this morning.

"Chris, come on. Just do it," Maggie begged, holding the crumpled note up to me. I was stretched out on my bed, trying to read *Brave New World*.

"If you're so interested, why don't you get all those ransom demands together?" I asked her, not looking up from my book.

"Could I please see the list?" asked Kayla. Maggie handed her the wrinkled piece of paper, and Kayla read the items off. "Eyedropper, mint-flavored dental floss, yellow-and-green-striped socks, Hello Kitty address book . . ." Kayla lowered the paper and looked around at everyone. "This is the strangest list of items I've ever seen."

"I have an eyedropper," said Maggie.

"I have a Hello Kitty address book!" Laurel-Ann yelled excitedly.

"Now how would the laundry ladies know that?" asked Boo with a shrug.

"Betsy has mint-flavored dental floss," said Maggie. "And Chris has yellow-and-green-striped socks! Don't you get it? We all have one item on the list!"

"Hey, yeah!" Shelby stood at the end of the bunk beds and grinned at me. "It's like the scavenger hunt from evening program!"

For evening program one night a while back, all of Middler Line had had a scavenger hunt, and each cabin was given a different list of items to hunt down. We'd had to find two live tadpoles, a Batman toothbrush, a Connecticut state quarter, a 1980 Pine Haven T-shirt, and about fifteen other random, bizarre items.

The crazy thing was, Betsy actually did have a Pine Haven T-shirt from 1980 because her mom had gone here back in the day, but we couldn't find a Batman toothbrush or a Connecticut state quarter, so Cabin Two ended up winning.

"Let's do it. It'll be fun," said Betsy, grabbing a clean pillowcase from the shelf by her bed and holding it open so everyone could start putting the items in.

"Wait a second, everyone. Gloria said we need to respect each other's belongings. She might not like that we're going along with this prank," said Laurel-Ann.

"Hyphen, who cares?" said Boo. "She and Wayward are at the staff meeting in Senior Lodge. Let's do it now while they're gone."

"Yeah, we have to. Poor Melvin is out there all alone, pants-less," said Maggie, and everyone laughed about that.

Meanwhile, I hadn't moved. I stared at the page in front of me, pretending to read. I'd kept my cool all day long, but now I could feel that hot lump of charcoal in my stomach flaring up into a glowing red coal again.

I was trying to be a good sport about this, but it wasn't fair. I really had been singled out. Everyone else's prank was over and done with as soon as it happened.

But not mine. No, mine had to be this elaborate, drawn-out *event* that involved everyone in the whole freaking cabin.

Maybe if I'd gotten the ransom note one minute and then found Melvin ten seconds later, the way

Betsy discovered her missing retainers, I might have laughed along with everyone else. But that hadn't happened. Why was I being picked on?

"Let me find my postcard from Myrtle Beach," Shelby said, racing over to Side B to get her contribution.

"My SpongeBob washcloth smells mildewy, but I'll put it in," offered Boo.

While everyone rushed around, I lay propped up on one elbow, my eyes scanning the page, but I hadn't read a single word.

Devon was behind all this. She had to be. It seemed like she was always nearby when each prank was first discovered. She'd been one of the first in the cabin that rainy day to find her "body." She'd been in the cabin all afternoon reading on the day the laundry came back.

She'd probably played the first prank on herself to throw us all off track, then planned out every other incident. She was a real mastermind that way. If anyone could pull all these pranks off, she could.

She went to crafts a lot when Maggie and I were canoeing, so she'd probably made Betsy's red lips. She'd always thought Wayward was so cool in her plaid hat, and even though she swore she couldn't thread a needle, it would take only a couple of stitches to attach the socks to Maggie's jersey.

But why wouldn't she have let me in on it? I was her *best* friend. Or at least I used to be. She could've told me all about it that day we were playing chess. Melvin's kidnapping could've been *our* joke.

I'd asked her point-blank that day if she was responsible for Maggie's prank, but she'd denied it. And yet she'd had this sly smile on her face. Like she knew something I didn't know. The whole time, I thought she was just figuring out her next chess move.

"Please be careful with this. I do want it back eventually," said Kayla, slipping a piece of her piano sheet music into the pillowcase.

I turned the page, staring so hard at the print that the letters seemed to vibrate with a pulsing movement. Devon had probably told Maggie her secret by now. I glanced at her standing there next to Betsy, a big smile on her face, her red locks hanging down in limp waves. Yep, she might even be in on this too.

And Devon. She sat perched on the edge of her bottom bunk, leaning forward a little. She seemed to love all the activity. *Look at this brilliant prank I've pulled off*, her expression seemed to say.

"The last item on the list is *Member of the Wedding?*" said Kayla, her voice rising in a question as she read from the paper.

"Oh, yeah! That's Devon's book she let me borrow," said Maggie, scrambling up to her top bunk and grabbing the paperback from her shelf. "Here you go." She tossed the book into the pillowcase Betsy held open, then turned around to Devon and gave her a fist bump.

"That's every item on the list," said Devon, smiling at Maggie.

Maggie was reading *Member of the Wedding*? Devon had said I could read it next.

The lump of charcoal in my stomach burst into flames. That proved it beyond the shadow of a doubt. They were in this together.

Betsy held the pillowcase up to me. "That's everything, Chris. You should probably go to the lodge on your own, don't you think? We don't want to scare away the bearnappers."

I sat up on my bunk and looked at them. "You're sure it's everything?" I asked calmly, but I could feel my heart pounding out a crazy drumbeat.

"It's everything on the list," said Kayla. I climbed down from my top bunk and took the pillowcase from Betsy. The second I had it in my hands, I had no idea what I'd do next—walk down to the lodge and get my bear back, dump all the items out on the floor and start yelling my head off, or maybe even go to Lakeview

Rock and toss the whole pillowcase over the edge into the water below.

I honestly didn't know myself what my next move was going to be. I clutched the pillowcase with one hand.

"Okay, everyone. I have an announcement to make." My heart felt like an atom bomb on the verge of explosion. "Devon's the one who's been doing this! She played the first prank on herself so we'd never suspect her."

The second I said that, I regretted it.

Devon's mouth was open so wide she looked like she could swallow a whole tomato without any effort at all.

"I did not! Chris! How can you say that?" she gasped.

Good question. Why was I always doing this—getting mad about something and then saying something I regretted?

I wished more than anything that I could force myself to laugh, say it was just a stupid joke, and then go to the lodge and get my bear back. I wanted all of this to be over.

But it was too late. Everyone was watching us, waiting to see what would happen next.

I couldn't believe what I was doing. I walked over to my duffel, unzipped it, and placed the pillowcase inside before zipping it back up again.

"I'm not going along with this, Devon. Go ahead and send Melvin back, little bits of stuffing at a time. I dare you," I said.

The whole cabin was silent, and I wanted more than anything for the cabin floor to open up into a big, yawning cavern and swallow me whole.

CHAPTER 23

Wednesday, July 9

I clutched the empty canvas laundry bag, trying to decide if I really wanted to go through with this. I was all alone in the cabin. Everyone else was at morning activities, including Devon and Maggie, who'd probably gone to tennis together or something. They'd hardly spoken to me since Sunday.

Devon and Maggie were always together now, and I wasn't even following along behind them anymore, listening to their vegetarian discussions. I'd never felt so lonely in my life.

If only I'd taken the pillowcase down to the lodge on Sunday evening. I would've gotten "further instructions" about where to find Melvin, and then this all would have been over.

If I'd done that Sunday night, then I wouldn't even be considering what I was about to do with this laundry bag.

But no. I'd had to drag it out for three days.

"Chris, just let me take the ransom items to the lodge for you," Betsy had begged me Sunday night after supper. Even then, I couldn't make myself laugh at the joke. I was still so mad about everything. And so embarrassed about the way I'd acted.

"Just stay out of this, Betsy," I'd warned her. "It's between Devon and me."

I never should've accused Devon of being behind all the pranks. Not without any real proof. Everyone else seemed to think it was Boo, but why would Boo play such a complicated prank on me? It didn't make sense.

But that was just the kind of thing Devon would think of, something really elaborate. Maybe I didn't have any actual proof, but it had to be Devon. It just had to be.

And now she was mad because I refused to go along with it. Yesterday she'd confronted me. "I can't believe how immature you're being. If you apologize for that false accusation you made, I *might* forgive you." Maggie stood beside her, not saying anything.

"Why don't you just give me my bear back? The joke's over," I told her.

Devon walked away without answering. If she really

was behind the bearnapping, I was positive she'd told Maggie by now.

That still made me mad every time I thought about it. Now they were both in on it together. Why would my friends be so mean about this and refuse to give me my bear back? They knew how mad I was. I felt like they were both punishing me for being a bad sport.

And yeah, okay—I was a bad sport. I wished more than anything I'd gone along with the joke on Sunday. But I hadn't.

So now I'd figured out a way to end this, and I was going to have the last laugh.

I glanced at Wayward's clock on the shelf by her bed. It was a little past ten. Earlier this morning I'd left a note on Devon's bed:

I'm sick and tired of this stupid prank.
I'm leaving the pillowcase on the back porch
of Middler Lodge at 11:00 today. There
better be "further instructions" waiting so
I can get my bear back.

Devon had found the note after breakfast. "I do not have your bear, Chris," she insisted, emphasizing each word.

"Whatever," I answered, trying to sound as calm and rational as she always did.

"Attention, everyone," Devon announced loudly to the whole cabin. "Chris, for whatever reason, suddenly decided this morning to finish what we started Sunday night. The time is eleven a.m., same location."

"What's going on?" asked Gloria suspiciously.

"Nothing, everything's fine," Betsy assured her.

I had plenty of time to carry out my plan. I was going to leave the ransom demands all right, but I was also going to play a prank of my own.

They have this coming to them, I told myself.

I took the bag over to Devon's black trunk and opened it first. All of her clothes were folded neatly inside. I scooped up an armful of stuff and shoved it into the laundry bag. I was so nervous my hands were shaking, and I kept dropping her clothes on the floor, but I worked quickly.

It took only a few minutes before Devon's trunk was completely empty and all her clothes were jammed into the laundry bag. I punched her clothes down inside it with my fists to make room for the next load.

I had to admit, I did feel a little guilty about this part. I was mostly mad at Devon, but Maggie *had* to be

Devon's partner by now. I was almost positive about that. And neither one of them had talked to me for the past two days.

So I moved over to Maggie's trunk and opened it up. I had to laugh, because hers was the opposite of Devon's. Nothing was folded; all her clothes were a wrinkled, unorganized mess. I grabbed a couple of armfuls of her clothes and packed them in on top of Devon's.

Something tapped against the window screen, and I jumped. I looked up and inspected the screen. A bug had crashed into it, and now it was banging its wings frantically to get loose from the mesh of the screen. I went back to work. Pretty soon I'd totally emptied out Maggie's trunk too, so I closed the lid and pushed the laundry bag out of the way.

I let out a slow breath. Now came the hardest part: hiding the evidence of my crime. I went to the door and took a quick look around. The coast was clear.

I grabbed the laundry bag and hoisted it over my shoulder. It wasn't as heavy as I thought it was going to be, but it was awfully bulky and kind of hard to carry. I walked out the door, heading down Middler Line.

If I saw anyone, I'd act like nothing was up; I'd just keep walking. If anyone asked me what I was doing,

I'd say I was taking our bag full of clean laundry to the cabin. Hopefully, no one would notice I was walking *away* from the cabin instead of *toward* it.

But luckily, I didn't see anyone. I walked all the way to the end of Middler Line and then veered off the path into the thick growth of trees and brush nearby. It was so overgrown here that I stumbled as I pushed through the tangle of vines and brush. Tree branches hit my face and arms as I lumbered along, dragging the canvas bag behind me. Dead leaves crunched underneath the weight of the bag.

I stopped and looked around. This seemed like a good place to leave it, here between these two trees. I piled some leaves and fallen branches around it so the whiteness of the bag wouldn't be visible from the path. Then I crashed back through the brush. Once I was out of the woods, I noticed I had a long scratch on my upper arm, but it wasn't bleeding.

I heard the sound of a screen door and glanced quickly toward Cabin One. I waited for a few seconds to see if anyone was coming out the door. When no one did, I took a deep breath. So far, so good. Looking back through the trees, I couldn't see any sign of the bag.

Now it was time for the next step. I walked back to our cabin and got the pillowcase of ransom demands from my duffel. Glancing at the clock, I saw that it was now 10:35. Plenty of time to drop this stuff off at the lodge.

When I got to the back porch, I wasn't quite sure what to do. I sort of expected to see Melvin sitting on one of the wooden benches or something, but there wasn't any sign of him. I stood around for a few seconds. Was I just supposed to leave the stuff and walk away?

I hated this! Why did Devon have to make my prank so complicated? I never would've gotten so mad if I'd had a simple prank played on me like everyone else.

But it didn't matter. She and Maggie had a little surprise of their own coming to them. If they didn't give Melvin back now that I'd gone through with the ransom demands, then they definitely deserved what I'd just done to them.

And if they did give me Melvin back . . . well, I'd tell them where their clothes were. Their missing clothes served as my insurance policy.

I dropped the pillowcase onto the wooden boards of the porch and sat down on a bench. Should I wait around?

Then I noticed a folded piece of paper stuck under the foot of the bench next to me. I pulled it out and read the printed message.

LEAVE THE ITEMS UNDER THIS BENCH. MELVIN IS WAITING FOR YOU ON THE ANGELHAIR FALLS TRAIL.

I shoved the pillowcase under the bench and took off at a run. The trail to Angelhair Falls started behind the camp office. I jogged the whole way. He'd better be in good shape, not all dirty or anything. Had he been left there since Saturday night? Nobody went on that trail unless there was a group taking a hike to the falls.

I passed the office and turned onto the path that led through the woods. Where was he exactly? In a tree? In the brush somewhere? I saw a flash of blue and ran faster. It was a person!

"Hey!" I yelled.

Blond hair, blue shirt, crashing through the trees off the side of the path. Trying to get away!

"Hey, stop! I can see you!"

She stopped running and turned slowly. A familiar face.

"Betsy?"

Betsy's face was flaming red. She clutched a pants-less Melvin against her chest.

"Uh . . . hi, Chris." She stared at me, and I saw her swallow hard. "You're—you're early."

"You're the bearnapper?"

Betsy took three steps backward and almost tripped over a fallen log. "I'm so sorry! It was just a joke. I didn't know what to do. You were so upset, and I didn't know all this was going to happen! I didn't mean to make you mad!"

I stared at her with my mouth hanging open. *Betsy.* I couldn't believe it.

"You wrote the ransom note?" I asked her.

Betsy's head bobbed up and down. Her eyes had a look of sheer terror in them. "I wrote the ransom note. I sewed the socks to Maggie's jersey, I constructed Devon's body, I switched out Wayward's hats. I even played a prank on myself." She took a few more steps backward. "I'm sorry. Don't be mad at me, okay?"

She looked like she was on the verge of tears. "You swear that Devon didn't have anything to do with this?" I asked.

She shook her head. "Devon didn't have a *thing* to do with this. Nothing! It was all me. All by myself."

I sat down on the path and clutched my head in my hands. Then I couldn't help it. I started to giggle. "You're the secret prankster!" I looked up at her. "How'd you pull all of that off?"

Betsy shrugged, and her shoulders relaxed a little. "Are you mad at me?"

"No. Just tell me how you did it!" The more I thought about how she'd fooled us all, the funnier it seemed. I covered my mouth because I couldn't stop giggling about it.

Betsy let out a slow breath. She seemed relieved that I wasn't going to blow up at her. For whatever reason, instead of making me mad, it was totally cracking me up to think that Betsy had been behind all this and we'd never once suspected her.

Betsy stepped through the brush so that she was on the path with me and handed me Melvin. He looked absolutely fine, except for the fact that he had no pants on.

"It just . . . happened. I never set out to play a prank on everyone in the cabin. One thing led to another."

Once Betsy got over her fear that she was going to be the latest target of my temper, she started talking. And boy, did she have a story to tell.

She told me that from the very first day, she'd felt left out because she was new and Maggie, Devon, and I already knew each other. "Everybody had a nickname but me," she complained.

On the day she'd played the first prank on Devon, it was raining, and she'd been all by herself in the cabin. She'd been thinking about how much Devon hated camp, so she'd written out "Devon's Top Ten Reasons for Hating Camp" to entertain herself.

"Then I thought I'd leave it on Devon's bed. But that seemed pretty boring by itself." So she'd gotten the idea for Devon's body from a skit that some people had done at her school with pillowcase faces.

"I was a little worried that Devon would get mad, but she didn't. And then everybody thought it was really funny, and nobody ever suspected me."

She hadn't planned on getting Maggie next, but she'd happened to be the first one to find the clean laundry that day, and when she saw Maggie's socks stuck to someone's shirt from the static cling, she'd come up with the idea for that prank.

"I made those goofy lips at crafts one day, and I was playing around with them when I noticed my retainer case on the shelf and . . . I don't know why I thought of it. I figured nobody would ever play a prank on me, so I played one on myself."

I couldn't stop laughing. "And by then, it was a huge mystery!"

"I know! And everybody thought the pranks were funny. Till the bear thing."

I sighed. "No, that was funny too. I just didn't have a sense of humor about it. And I was absolutely convinced it was Devon."

"I'm really sorry, Chris. I didn't mean to make you mad, and then . . . I didn't know what to do! Give the bear back? Leave another note? Confess?"

Betsy paced back and forth on the path in front of me, running her hands through her short hair. "I was going to give you Melvin back on Saturday night after you got mad, but I was scared to death you'd catch me returning him. It got out of control!"

"Oh my God!" I looked up at Betsy. "I just remembered! Betsy, you've got to help me! Something else is about to get out of control!"

CHAPTER 24

"What? What's wrong?" Betsy asked me when I jumped to my feet and took off running down the path.

"I did something—something mean to Devon and Maggie because I thought they were the ones who'd kidnapped Melvin," I told her as she raced to catch up with me. "I emptied everything from both their trunks into the laundry bag earlier and hid it in the woods!"

Betsy let out a nervous laugh. "Oh, wow! We'd better hurry!"

"I know, right? Just think how mad they're going to be when they find two completely empty trunks. I thought they had it coming to them. How did I know they're both innocent?" As worried as I was about undoing my prank, the whole thing was pretty funny, and I couldn't stop laughing.

We jogged past the camp office and almost ran right into Eda, who was carrying her always-present clipboard. "Well, good morning, ladies. Nice day for a run," she called to us as we sprinted past her.

I threw her a friendly wave, and when she was out of earshot, I glanced at Betsy. "Think she suspects that we've both committed felonies?"

Betsy snorted with laughter. "Maybe she'll come visit us in lockup!"

"Stop laughing!" I told her, but I couldn't make myself stop. "We've really got to fix this. ¡Vámos, chica! We have to hurry!"

We ran up the steep hill to Middler Line. We were both panting and out of breath by the time we got to the place where I'd dragged the canvas bag into the woods.

"This way, but be careful. I got scratched up by the tree branches before," I warned Betsy as we struggled through the brush. I stopped when I came to the two trees.

"Wait a second," I said, looking around. The bag was nowhere in sight.

"What's wrong?" asked Betsy, standing behind me. She was still breathing heavily from our jog up the hill.

"It's gone," I said finally. My eyes were scanning every

inch of ground around us, but the bag wasn't there.

"Maybe this isn't where you left it," Betsy suggested, wiping the sweat off her forehead with the side of her arm. Her hair was stuck in wet strands against her bright pink face.

"No. It was right here!" I pointed to the mashed-down leaves and underbrush on the ground around us. "See, you can tell that's where I dragged it along." I patted the two tree trunks in front of me. "Then I shoved it right in between these trees and covered it up with those leaves and branches."

I saw something white under the dead leaves I was pointing to and kicked it with my foot. It was a sock.

"Evidence!" I shouted, picking up the sock. I spun around in a circle, looking in all directions for any sign of the bag. "I'm telling you, Betsy—someone must have moved it!"

"Okay, so first the bear is kidnapped, now the clothes?" Betsy said slowly, trying to take it all in.

"Let's look around some more."

We spent probably fifteen minutes scrambling through that thick section of woods, but the laundry bag was gone.

"Poof!" I said, holding my hands up. "It's like it disappeared into thin air!"

"Maybe Devon and Maggie saw you and brought their stuff back after you left," Betsy said.

I clutched Melvin under one arm and held the stray sock in my other hand. "I was really careful not to let anybody see me." I looked at Betsy. "What am I going to do now?"

Betsy shook her head. "This is all my fault."

"Stop it!" I snapped, and Betsy looked worried that I was going to blow my top at her. "I mean, *I* did this. You can't blame yourself. You didn't know anything about this."

"Now what?" asked Betsy.

"I guess we go back to the cabin," I said, not looking forward to what was about to happen. "I have to face this sometime."

We made our way through the brush back out onto Middler Line. Maybe Maggie and Devon wouldn't be in the cabin yet. Or if they were, maybe they hadn't yet looked in their trunks.

But I'd have to tell them. They'd find out eventually.

Betsy opened the door to the cabin, and we walked in to find Devon standing next to her open, empty trunk.

Maggie was inside her own trunk with her knees folded up. She reminded me of someone sitting in an old-fashioned bathtub.

"Okay, Chris, what's going on?" Devon snapped as soon as she saw me.

"Yeah," said Maggie from inside the trunk, "first a bearnapping. Now a robbery."

Betsy stood with her hands clasped in front of her and cleared her throat. "You know, this used to be a really nice neighborhood before the recent crime wave." She looked at us all solemnly. "Maybe we should start a block watch."

Betsy sounded so serious, I couldn't help myself. I covered my face with both hands and started laughing. Pretty soon, my whole body was shaking with laughter. "Okay . . . okay, this isn't funny," I said, but I couldn't control myself. "This isn't funny, and I promise I'm going to fix it."

I was trying to get my story out, but I couldn't stop laughing. I tried to catch my breath, but the sight of Maggie sitting in her empty trunk and Devon standing there looking so annoyed and Betsy looking so serious made me start up all over again.

Devon sighed. "She's delirious."

"You got Melvin back!" Maggie noticed suddenly. "Put his pants back on."

That comment made me fall to my knees. Here Maggie and Devon were, both missing every piece of clothing they had, and yet Maggie was concerned about my pants-less teddy bear. I laughed so hard, I was afraid I was going to wet my pants.

Now Maggie and Betsy were both laughing too. I took the stray white sock I'd been clutching in my hand and draped it over Melvin's bare bottom.

"Is that better?" I said finally, gasping for breath.

"Wait a second, is that my sock?" Devon asked. She took two steps forward and snatched it off of Melvin. That almost killed the rest of us. We laughed for another five minutes at least while Devon stood there, sighing and shaking her head.

"Let me explain," I said, taking deep breaths and wiping my face. "I did something really mean. I put all your clothes in the laundry bag and hid the bag in the woods." I'd finally stopped laughing, and now it was time to get serious.

"I was convinced you'd kidnapped Melvin and I was just trying to get back at you." Devon frowned at me, waiting for me to go on. "But . . . then I found out Betsy was the one who kidnapped Melvin, so she was going to help me put your stuff back."

Devon had a disgusted look on her face. "I don't understand this endless fascination with ridiculous pranks!" She narrowed her eyes at me. "So where are all my clothes?"

"That's a really good question. I wish I knew." I told them about how Betsy and I had gone back to the woods to get the laundry bag, but it was missing.

"Chris, I can't believe you did this," Devon said. She sounded so annoyed, but I had to admit she was taking it surprisingly well. Much better than I would have, that was for sure.

Meanwhile, Maggie hadn't moved from her trunk. She didn't seem the least bit upset that all of her clothes had disappeared.

"I have an announcement to make. I want to say something," I started. "I've—I wish I could . . ." They were all three looking at me, and I couldn't think of how to get the words out. "What I mean is . . . *lo siento mucho.*"

There, I'd said it. Finally.

Devon looked at me and waited. Maggie gripped the sides of her trunk. Betsy stood there with a confused little smile on her face.

"And I really mean that," I assured them, because they didn't seem too impressed that I'd just apologized.

"Mean what?" asked Maggie. "What did you say?"

"I said I was sorry!"

"Oh," said Maggie. "No wonder you don't apologize very often. You really suck at it."

Everyone burst out laughing over that, including Devon.

"I'm sorry! *¡Lo siento!*" I yelled over their laughter. "*¡Es mi culpa!* It's all my fault! There—is that any better?"

At that moment Boo walked in the door and stared at Maggie. "What are you doing?"

"Packing," Maggie said simply.

Boo shrugged and went over to Side B. Then she came back over and gave us all a puzzled look. "Didn't we already sort the laundry?" she asked.

"What do you mean?" asked Betsy suspiciously.

Boo pointed toward the other side of the cabin. "There's another bag of laundry in the middle of the floor there."

At that, Maggie hopped out of her trunk in a single bound, and we all rushed over to see what Boo was talking about.

"That's it!" I shouted. The canvas laundry bag was sitting right in the middle of the floor on Side B.

"How did it get here?" asked Betsy.

"What's going on?" asked Boo.

"Great. Put my stuff back, please," Devon told me.

I crouched down and examined the bottom of the bag. "Everyone, look! See how there's dirt on the bottom of the bag? And that's a grass stain! Somebody moved this after I hid it!" I turned to Betsy. "Are you sure you're not the mastermind behind this?"

"No! I had absolutely nothing to do with this, cross my heart."

I peeked inside the bag. It was crammed full of all the clothes I'd shoved in it earlier. I let out a huge, relieved sigh. I'd never been so happy to see piles of clean laundry in my life.

"Okay, I have *no* idea what's going on, but Melvin's back, your missing clothes are back, and I gave you all a really lousy apology. So I'd say everything's okay now!"

CHAPTER 25

Friday, July 11

I sat on my top bunk and paused for a few seconds, holding my pen above the paper. Rest hour was almost over, so I had to finish this up fast. My hand was feeling cramped from all the writing I'd done, but it was worth it. When I was finished, I reread the letter I'd just written.

> Maggie,
> I know I really suck at apologies, but here goes. I feel really bad for the way I treated you when we broached on that rock. I don't want to remind you of all the mean things I said, so I'll just say, "*Lo siento.*" I'm sorry. And I'm sorry I yelled at you the night Melvin

got kidnapped, and sorry I blamed you for it.
One more thing: Thanks for being so easygoing
about the prank I played on you. How's that?
Am I getting better?

Chris

I folded her letter up into a paper airplane and wrote
her name on the wing. Then I checked over the letter to
Devon again.

Devon,

There are so many things I feel bad about.
Maggie told me I suck at apologies, but maybe
the more I do this, the better I'll get at it.

My Top Five List of Things I'm Sorry I
Did to My Best Friend, Devon

1. Rubbing it in that you're not bilingual
YET (but you can get really good at Spanish,
and I'll teach you new words)

2. Not talking to you for DAYS after
the first dance

3. Accusing you of kidnapping Melvin

4. Emptying out your trunk and hiding
your clothes

5. Calling you a horrible friend because

you talked to Jackson (you're not—you're
definitely my BEST friend)
    I just want to say *Lo siento.* I'm sorry
for all these things.
    Chris

Then I folded Devon's letter into a paper airplane
too and wrote her name on the wing. I leaned over to
look at her on the bunk below me. "Hey, incoming," I
said before I sent the airplane sailing down to her.

Once Devon had caught her note, I flew Maggie's
note across the cabin, and it landed at the foot of her
bed. I lay stretched out on my bunk, looking up at the
rafters. I knew they were both reading their notes now
because I'd heard them unfolding the paper.

I did feel better. A lot better. I still didn't like admitting I was wrong about stuff, but at least I was learning
a little bit at a time. And I figured my temper would get
me in trouble again sometime, but I'd decided I really,
really needed to work on controlling it.

The past few days of camp had been just about
perfect. Finally, all three of us were friends with each
other at the same time. We'd gone to activities together,
Devon was teaching Maggie how to play chess, and I'd
even been eating the vegetarian choices at meals since

Wednesday. Maybe I wasn't ready to give up meat completely, but it made Devon happy when I ate the veggie lasagna last night instead of pork chops.

I heard the bell ringing for the end of rest hour, so I sat up and noticed that Maggie had finished reading her note and was carefully refolding it back into a paper airplane. "Hey, Kachina, I totally forgive you. I'd say you're definitely getting better at the whole apology thing. Good job."

"You think so?" I asked, climbing down from my bunk. "That's a relief." I looked at Devon. "How about my other best friend? Do you totally forgive me too?"

"*Other* best friend?" Devon raised her eyebrows. "I'm not sure I like the sound of that."

"Hey, we've all been getting along great lately, so don't stir things up," I warned her. "Do you forgive me or not?"

Devon folded up her apology note and laid it on the shelf by her bed. "I suppose I can forgive you. Oh, wipe that wounded look off your face. Of course I forgive you."

Betsy was about to walk out the door behind Shelby and Boo when I called to her. "Hey, Mastermind! Come back here for a second."

Betsy smiled at her new nickname and came back inside.

"I was thinking—we should all sign our names somewhere on the wall. All the Side A girls, okay?" I went to my duffel and dug around inside it for the bottle of black shoe polish I'd bought before camp started. I'd packed it for just this purpose.

"Here it is. This is how we'll really leave our mark." I pulled out the bottle and shook it up.

Devon stared at the graffiti-covered walls all around us. "There aren't any blank spots left," she insisted.

"How about down here?" I asked. I pushed the end of our bunk beds away from the wall and pointed to a spot that was almost completely untouched.

"Nobody can see it there because the bunks are in the way," said Maggie.

"No, this'll be perfect," I told her. "There's room for all four of us." I kept shaking the bottle to get the polish mixed up. "How about we sign our nicknames?" I suggested.

Then I took the cap off the bottle and wrote "Kachina" with the sponge tip before handing the bottle to Maggie.

"Hmm, which name should I sign? Windsoroni, Beefaroni, Veggeroni?"

"Don't forget King Kong, Gorilla Feet, or Banana Eater," added Devon.

"I guess I'll pick my favorite—which would have to be Beefaroni, the name my *best* friend Devon gave me on the first day of camp," Maggie said with a grin.

When she finished, she handed the bottle to Devon, who acted totally bored with this whole ritual. "Same thing for me—which name? Ghosty Girl, Grainy Girl, or Palechild?" She sighed, but she could hardly keep from smiling. She leaned forward and wrote "Palechild," making the letters as fancy as she could with the sponge tip.

"Last but certainly not least—Mastermind. You're next," I said as Devon passed the black bottle to Betsy, who was grinning from ear to ear.

Betsy signed her new nickname and then put the cap back on the bottle. The strong smell of shoe polish filled the air.

"Kachina, Beefaroni, Palechild, Mastermind," I read off the list. "That's gonna make future Pine Haven campers wonder, don't you think?"

"Thanks, everyone," said Betsy. "I don't feel like such a newbie anymore."

"Hey, I still can't believe a newbie was the one who was pranking everyone in the cabin," said Maggie. "Newbies never play pranks!"

"Well, yeah," said Betsy, "but remember, my mom came to Pine Haven for seven years, and she told me all kinds of stories about the pranks they used to play. I kept expecting to be short-sheeted every single night, but . . . nothing. Nobody was playing pranks on anyone, at least in this cabin."

"To me, it seemed like there were constant pranks," said Devon. "Underwear hanging from the flagpole one morning, *pink* underwear after the Camp Crockett dance." She shook her head. "It's so ridiculous."

Maggie looked at Betsy suspiciously. "I still think you had help. Did Wayward put you up to this? How did you know where to find a top hat, for crying out loud?"

Betsy smiled bashfully. "Haven't you ever gone to Junior Lodge? I just went over there one day when I had nothing else to do and found that big trunk full of costumes."

"You're a Mastermind, no doubt about it," I told her.

"This has been a really fun summer," Betsy said. "I'm definitely coming back next year. Is anyone else?"

"I'll be back next year. And Chris, too. We'll be CATs and then counselors together someday, right? All of us will," Maggie said, looking around at everyone.

"No way," Devon said, shaking her head. "Once I escape from this backwoods camp tomorrow, I'm never coming back again. I can't wait to get back to the civilized world!"

"Grainy Girl, how can you say that? If you don't come back next year, you and I won't ever see each other again," said Maggie. She frowned and cupped her chin in her hands.

A surprised look spread across Devon's face. She seemed to just now realize we'd be saying good-bye to Maggie tomorrow. "Yeah, but . . . you can come and visit Chris and me. Maybe over the winter break."

"I'll come back next year," I told Maggie, because she looked so depressed. "And I'll work on getting Devon to come with me."

Devon sighed. "Four weeks of this torturous place again? You know how miserable I've been this past month! Listen, everyone has an open invitation to come to my house anytime. We have electricity and indoor plumbing. You'll love it."

"Just wait till after the Circle Fire tonight," I told Devon. "The last campfire is so sad, you'll be crying your eyes out and counting down the days till you can come back to Pine Haven next year."

"Ha!" said Devon.

"Just wait," I assured her.

CHAPTER 26

Saturday, July 12

"Grainy Girl, stop crying. You'll smear your mascara." Maggie handed Devon another Kleenex.

Devon dabbed at her eyelashes with it. "I'm not usually so emotional." She looked around at all the Cabin Four girls gathered around us, waiting to say good-bye before we got on the bus.

"Keep in touch, okay?" she said finally. We'd been hugging everyone and crying for at least twenty minutes, it seemed, but now we really had to get on the bus. The doors were about to close.

"Bye, Christina Kachina." Maggie gave me one last hug, and both of us laughed at how runny our noses were. I turned around to get on the bus, but Gloria stopped me.

"Here, maybe this will give you a laugh," she said, pressing a piece of paper into my pocket. Then she hugged me, and Eda, who was standing by with her clipboard, gave me a little pat to get me moving up the bus steps.

I followed Devon down the aisle of the bus. We picked seats near the front, shoving our pillows and Devon's overnight bag into the storage bins overhead.

"If JD sings the whole way home like she did on the trip up here, I might need that pillow to cover her face with," said Devon, still sniffling.

"You have to admit she was good in the talent show." I sank into the seat beside Devon. All the crying I'd been doing since last night left me feeling washed out.

"She was mildly amusing. Kayla was amazing on the piano, wasn't she?"

"Yeah, she was," I agreed. I didn't feel like I'd gotten to know the Side B girls that well this summer, but Kayla had surprised me by saying she'd keep in touch with all of us this year.

"I've made some great friends at Pine Haven, and I want to keep them forever," she'd said tearfully at breakfast this morning.

"See—I knew you'd cry during the Circle Fire last night," I told Devon, who kept dabbing her eyes with the Kleenex. "You can't even stop now."

"I can too," she insisted. "It wasn't all those corny songs and speeches about sisterhood and friendship that got to me last night."

"Oh, really?" I said. "What was it then? Smoke in your eyes?" Just about everyone cried at the final campfire. Even counselors cried. How could you spend four weeks with the same group of girls and not be sad to say good-bye to all of them?

"Well, don't laugh. I really liked how at the end, Eda lit that candle from the campfire, and then passed the flame around to light up all of our candles. And afterward, we all sat there in the dark, holding our candles and singing. That part was nice."

"Yeah, I love that part too," I agreed. I'd saved my candle stub from last night.

The bus had pulled out of camp now and was turning onto the highway. I could feel us speeding up, and lots of girls were sobbing as we left Pine Haven behind.

"Hey, I want to ask you something," I said to Devon, staring ahead at the seat in front of me. "You know how I lose my temper so much? Do you think there's something wrong with me?"

Devon sighed. "Of course not. You're just a hothead."

"Oh, wow, thanks. That makes me feel better. Seriously—I'm kind of worried about it."

Devon was quiet for a minute, and I could tell she was giving her answer some serious thought. "Here's how I look at it. You have brown eyes, perfect teeth, and a short fuse. It's a part of who you are, and you'll always be that way. Yes, maybe you can learn to control it. But you'll never be as laid-back as Wayward. That's just not you."

"You think so?" I asked, feeling a little better.

"Yes, I do. Take me, for instance. I don't have perfect teeth, and that's why I'll be experiencing the joy of braces next month. I need to straighten my teeth, and you need to work on your temper. But you are getting better."

"You're not just saying that?" I asked.

"No, I'm not. Sure you got mad quite a bit this summer, but I also noticed the times you kept your cool."

I took a deep breath. I was glad to hear that. "Want a piece of gum?" I asked Devon, reaching into my pocket for it. I felt something else and pulled it out to examine it.

"Oh yeah, I forgot! Gloria gave this to me," I told Devon as I unfolded the piece of paper.

Chris,

You were a good friend to help Devon and Maggie with their "laundry" this week. But you never know who might be watching! Hope to see you next summer.

Gloria

"Oh my gosh, Devon! Gloria was the one who brought the laundry bag back!" I poked her in the ribs and showed her the note. "She never let on she knew a single thing about it." I laughed, thinking how I never gave Gloria that much credit as a new counselor this summer, but she'd fooled me till the last minute.

Devon groaned. "I admit, I'm going to miss Gorilla Feet, but I'm not going to miss all those childish pranks!"

I turned away from her and gazed out the window, trying not to let her see me laugh. Maybe tonight I'd have to sneak into her room and short-sheet her bed.

Just a little way to welcome her home.

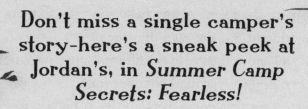

Don't miss a single camper's story—here's a sneak peek at Jordan's, in *Summer Camp Secrets: Fearless!*

When we went outside, Maddy was leaning against the car with this know-it-all look on her face. Not quite a smile, but almost.

The first thing she said was, "Did you throw up?"

"No." I brushed past her and climbed into the backseat.

"I swear, Jordan, you're the only one I know who gets carsick before you even leave the driveway." She scooted in next to me.

"I did not throw up! And excuse me for not being born perfect like *some* people." I stared out my window at the snowball bush by the driveway so I could avoid looking at her.

"You're excused!" She said it all perky. She was always in a good mood. I slightly hated her for that personality flaw.

Being too perky and perfect were just about the only personality flaws my sister had. She was sixteen, she made straight As, she was the star of her field hockey team, and about thirty-seven different boys were in love with her. And *nothing* made her nervous.

Perfection in older sisters has been known to cause regurgitation issues in younger sisters. I was fairly sure that medical studies had proven that.

Maddy fished through her purse, pulled out a stick of gum, and offered it to me. I shook my head. She unwrapped it and shoved it under my nose, but I ignored her. The snowball bush had my undivided attention.

Eric and Mama were climbing into the front seat.

Eric turned the engine on and peeked at us in the rearview mirror. "Ready, ladies?" My stepfather was the sweetest guy in the world. It drove him slightly crazy living in a houseful of females, but he always put up with it.

"Ready!" yelled perky, perfect Madison. She'd given up trying to get me to take the gum and was chewing it herself. We started backing out of the driveway.

We didn't have far to go, just down the street to my best friend Molly's house. Molly threw open the front door and raced down her steps the second we pulled in the driveway.

"Finally! I didn't think you'd ever get here!" She had her sleeping bag under one arm and her pillow under the other. Her parents came out, carrying Molly's trunk by the handles.

"Think we'll get all this gear in?" asked Molly's father when Eric opened our already full trunk. The two of them shifted the duffels, trunks, and bags around while Molly gave her mother one last hug.

Molly squeezed in between me and Madison. Good. We needed a barrier between us. Too bad the Great Wall of China wouldn't fit in the backseat.

"How many times did you throw up this morning?" she whispered.

"Zero! And I slightly hate you for even bringing it up," I whispered back.

Molly laughed. "See, you're getting better. I'm glad you didn't get sick. I almost called you to ask."

In lots of ways, Molly and I are complete opposites. She has brown eyes and super-straight brown hair cut really short and parted in the middle. I have blue eyes, and my blond hair is past my shoulders, with a little bit of curl to it. She's short and stocky; I'm taller and slimmer.

The fathers were finished packing the trunk, so they slammed it closed, and Molly's parents leaned into the open car door and took another ten minutes saying good-bye. Finally we were ready to leave.

After he got in, Eric turned around in the front seat and smiled at all of us. "Next stop, Camp Pine Haven for Girls!" He was the only one in the car who hadn't made a comment about my regurgitation issue. I loved him for that.

We backed out of Molly's driveway and headed down the street. My stomach felt completely normal now. Hopefully, it wouldn't turn on me later. It's truly sad when you can't even trust your own organs, but my stomach has betrayed me many times. I've learned the hard way to be suspicious of it.

Mama glanced over her shoulder at me. "Feeling okay, honey?" she asked with her forehead crinkled up in worry lines. "We'll turn the air conditioner on and get some cool air blowing on you, all right?"

I leaned my head back against the seat and closed my eyes. "I'm *fine*."

I hated the way everyone had to pay so much attention to me. But that was partly my fault for being so abnormal. I have never been good at dealing with new experiences, and it had been a really big deal for me to go away to summer camp in the first place.

At least no one had said anything about the "major

meltdown" summer. That was one of the worst experiences of my life.

Two years ago when I was ten, I was all set to go to camp for the first time. Eda Thompson, one of Mama's best friends, is the director of Pine Haven, so how could my mother have two daughters and not send them to her best friend's summer camp?

Madison had started going to camp when she was eight, and she loved everything about Pine Haven. So of course, everyone expected me to be just like Madison, but I didn't want to go when I was eight. Or nine.

Finally when I was ten, I felt this huge amount of pressure to go. I didn't want to, but I knew Mama, Madison, and Eda were all expecting me to go, and they all kept saying, "Just wait till you get there. You'll love it!"

But about fifty different things worried me. It was for a whole month, so I knew I'd be homesick, even with Maddy there and with Eda looking out for me. I'd be sleeping in a strange bed, away from home. I'd have to swim in a lake that was really deep with water that was dark green and you couldn't see the bottom of it. There would be all these strange girls I wouldn't know. Maybe my counselor would be really mean.

So about a week before camp started, I had a slight meltdown.

Actually, it was more like a major meltdown.

I started crying and I didn't stop. I cried for about two whole days. Major, major waterworks.

Everyone tried to comfort me in various ways that did absolutely no good at all. And yes, there were some regurgitation episodes. Eventually Mama said, "Fine, you don't have to go. You can stay home and miss out on all the fun."

So I stopped crying and immediately felt better, but I could tell she was majorly disappointed in me. Half of me felt so incredibly relieved that I didn't have to go to camp, but the other half felt like the biggest failure in the world.

So last summer when I was eleven, I knew I couldn't back out of it again. Luckily, Molly had moved to our neighborhood at the beginning of fifth grade and we got to be best, best friends. She wanted to go with me last year, and she was so excited that she made me feel a lot better about camp, but I was still nervous in the beginning.

Molly elbowed me and grinned. "Just think, tomorrow we'll actually be riding horses again! I can't wait to see Merlin. I wonder if he'll remember me."

Molly and I loved horseback riding more than any other activity at Pine Haven. Listening to her talk about horses made me excited. Camp really was fun, even if I did get nervous about the first day.

"I wonder if Amber will be in our cabin," said Molly.

"I don't know, but Eda promised she'd put you and me together."

I felt a sinking feeling inside me when I said that. Eda probably thought I would have another meltdown if Molly wasn't right by my side. Once you've had one meltdown, people keep expecting you to have additional ones.

Mama was always telling people, "Jordan is a little more cautious than Madison. Jordan needs a little more encouragement than Madison does. Jordan is more sensitive than Madison."

Translation: Madison is perfectly normal. Then there's my abnormal daughter.

Last summer I had managed to get through the whole month of camp without having a meltdown. But like that was a big deal.

This summer I had to do more than just survive camp. Last year, the day we got home, I heard Mama on the phone to Daddy, giving him a report of how things went. They've been divorced since I was five, but they still get along really well.

"Jordan survived!" I heard her telling him. Her

voice sounded so relieved. "Yes, she made it through the whole session. I honestly thought Eda was going to call me and say we'd have to come get her, but she made it! She survived! Maddy? Oh, well, you know how Madison loves camp. She thrived, just like she always does."

After I'd overheard that conversation, I went to my room and locked the door. I cried for an hour. *Jordan survived; Madison thrived.* It was a horrible rhyme stuck in my head that kept repeating itself over and over and over.

This summer, I couldn't just survive.

This summer, I wanted it to be my turn to thrive.